VICTORIA SCHWAB

everyday angel

Second Chances

SCHOLASTIC INC.

To Court, for the kindness.

No part of this publication may be reproduced, stored in a retrieval system, or transmitted in any form or by any means, electronic, mechanical, photocopying, recording, or otherwise, without written permission of the publisher. For information regarding permission, write to Scholastic Inc., Attention: Permissions Department, 557 Broadway, New York, NY 10012.

ISBN 978-0-545-52847-4

Copyright © 2014 by Victoria Schwab

All rights reserved. Published by Scholastic Inc. SCHOLASTIC and associated logos are trademarks and/or registered trademarks of Scholastic Inc.

12 11 10 9 8 7 6 5 4 3 2 1   14 15 16 17 18 19/0

Printed in the U.S.A.   40
First edition, September 2014

Book design by Yaffa Jaskoll

chapter 1

CAROLINE

The lunchroom at Westgate School for Girls was like a solar system.

Except instead of being full of planets and moons, it was full of uniformed girls and tables and noise. The school went from sixth grade to eighth grade, and each grade had their own separate lunchtime. Right now, it was the seventh grade's turn, and all sixty-three girls were orbiting the twelve cafeteria tables.

Caroline Mason stood clutching her tray and watching the other girls head toward their tables, drawn by the gravitational pull of friends and laughter and routine. She felt like she was drifting in space.

Everyone had a table. Caroline *used* to have a table.

She reached absently for the pendant that used to hang around her neck — a small half circle — before she remembered it wasn't there. She'd shoved it into the bottom drawer of the jewelry box on her bathroom counter.

Caroline knew she couldn't just stand there, so she took a deep breath and made her way to Table 12. Nobody sat at Table 12. Correction: nobody except for Caroline. She tried to keep her eyes on her tray, tried not to let anyone see how alone she felt as she walked.

But halfway there, her eyes floated up, drawn automatically to Table 7. To Lily Pierce.

If Westgate *were* a solar system, then Lily Pierce would be its sun.

With her perfect black curls and her perfect smile that seemed to make the whole lunch room lean toward her. And away from Caroline. Because everybody listened to Lily Pierce. Everybody did what she said. Whether or not they wanted to be her friend, they definitely *didn't* want to be her enemy. And Lily Pierce had told the entire seventh grade to stay away from Caroline Mason.

Lily and Caroline were at war. Only, Caroline didn't want to fight. She just wanted to go back to the way things were before. Back to before they were enemies.

Back to when they were best friends.

•   •   •

"Pick a hand," said Lily.

It was two years ago — summertime, and they were ten. They sat cross-legged on Caroline's trampoline. Lily had moved to their town of Beachwood, California, the year before — into the house right next door — but it felt like they'd been friends forever. Like they'd always be friends. They were starting sixth grade at Westgate together in the fall. They hadn't met Erica yet. Right now, it was just the two of them.

Caroline squinted at Lily's outstretched hands, skeptical. Lily liked to play tricks on people.

"Come on," Lily urged, nodding at her closed fists. "Pick one."

Caroline chewed her lip, and chose left. Lily smiled and turned up her hand. In her palm was a necklace with a silver half circle pendant on the end. Lily then turned over her other hand to reveal a matching necklace with a matching half circle.

"See, they fit together like this," said Lily, linking the pieces so they became a whole circle, like a moon. She looked proud of herself. "We have to wear them," she said. "And we can't ever take them off."

"Not ever?"

Lily shook her head, curls bobbing. "We can't take them off as long as we're friends, which will be forever, so no, not ever. If we take them off, the spell will break."

Caroline crinkled her nose. "What spell?"

"This one." Lily held out the necklace, palm up. "Put your hand over it." And Caroline did. "I solemnly swear," started Lily, giving Caroline a look that told her to repeat the words.

"I solemnly swear," Caroline echoed.

"That as long as I wear this."

"That as long as I wear this."

"I am half of a whole."

"I am half of a whole."

Lily beamed. She handed Caroline her silver pendant. "You look out for me," she said, "and I'll look out for you. And we'll stick together no matter what."

Caroline smiled, and slipped the necklace over her head. "No matter what."

Lily laughed, and the sound traveled through the lunchroom, jarring Caroline out of the memory.

Lily was sitting with Erica Kline and Whitney Abel. Every time Lily laughed, Erica echoed. She smiled when Lily smiled, pouted when Lily pouted, and tossed her straight brown hair when Lily tossed her black curls. She was like a clone, but meaner.

When Lily put her arms around Whitney and Erica's shoulders, it drove a spike through Caroline's stomach. In a way, all of this was Whitney's fault. And she didn't even know it. On the first day of school, Whitney had been nothing. Nobody. A girl with two dull brown braids who barely spoke. Now she was sitting at Table 7, Lily's newest pet.

Whitney said something, and Lily threw back her head and laughed again (a moment later, Erica laughed, too). Then they both leaned in. They were hunched forward over their table, working on something Caroline couldn't see.

Caroline tried to focus on her food, but she wasn't very hungry. She could feel the eyes of Table 7 flicking her way. She didn't want them to see how miserable she was, so she pretended to read through a notebook while the clock on the wall ticked off the minutes until she could go to class. Finally, when the first of the seventh graders started to leave, she pushed to her feet and went to return her tray to the carts by the door.

And that's when it happened.

As Caroline walked by Table 7, Lily pushed back her chair, blocking Caroline's path and forcing her to stop so fast she nearly spilled her tray. She caught it in time, and backed up, straight into Erica.

Or rather, Erica's *tray*.

Erica snickered, and Caroline felt something thick and wet run down the back of her uniform. Caroline turned to see Erica holding her tray not in front of her like a normal person, but up on its side so the whole flat surface was turned toward Caroline. It was covered in a horrible ugly swirl of ketchup and mustard and mayonnaise.

And now, so was Caroline.

The room went quiet as sixty-two pairs of eyes turned toward Caroline and her ruined uniform. Lily smiled. Erica mimicked her. Whitney watched, wide-eyed and silent.

"Ewwwww," said Erica, dropping her tray back on the table. "I got ketchup on my hands."

Lily held out a napkin. "Here you go."

"Thanks," said Erica, wiping her fingers and looking into Caroline's eyes. "Nobody wants to smell like a dirty lunch tray all day."

A glob of ketchup dripped onto Caroline's leg. Her eyes began to burn.

Don't cry, she thought desperately. *Don't cry. Don't cry.*

Lily watched her intently, waiting to see what she would do. Caroline wanted to sob. She wanted to scream. She wanted to punch Erica in the face. Instead she turned, dropped her tray off on the cart, and stormed through the doors, wishing she never had to come back.

chapter 2

ARIA

The shadow took shape on the steps of the school, between two manicured hedges. At first the shadow was just a blot on the stairs, but soon it spread, growing until it resembled the outline of a twelve-year-old girl.

A twelve-year-old *guardian angel*, to be exact.

A breeze blew past, rustling the bushes on either side. The shadow's outfit fluttered, too, and an instant later the whole shape filled with light, and a form rose up out of it. A girl stood there, wavy red hair falling down her back, her shoes resting on top of the pool of light.

Aria blinked and looked around. She had no idea where she was, but she knew *who* she was — still herself — and for that she was thankful.

"Good shadow," she said, and the light under her feet went out.

She nested her heels in the shadow's shoes, and realized as she looked down that she wasn't wearing the clothes she'd had on before. No blue leggings. No green sweater. No pink laces.

Instead, she was wearing a school uniform. White polo, plaid skirt, white knee socks, and black Oxford shoes. The polo had a crest over the pocket with a *W* embroidered on it.

Aria looked up at the stone mantel above the school's massive doors. It read:

WESTGATE PREPARATORY

. . . and in smaller print beneath it:

SCHOOL FOR GIRLS.

Aria's blue charm bracelet still dangled from her wrist, a single silver feather hanging from the first loop. That charm represented Gabby, the first girl Aria had helped. Two rings still hung empty, and as Aria gazed up at the front doors, she felt a little thrill of excitement. Someone here, at this school, was waiting for her, even though she didn't know it. Whoever it was, she would be marked for Aria, wreathed in smoke the same color as Aria's bracelet. And all Aria had to do was find her, and help her, and once she did, she'd be one step closer to earning her wings. When she squinted down at her shadow, she could almost see them. Just the beginnings, of course — a curve here, a feather there — but everyone had to start somewhere.

And today, Aria was starting here. At Westgate.

As Aria climbed the stairs, she considered her shoelaces. They were black, like the Oxfords they were threaded through. Aria chewed her lip. A little color couldn't hurt. As soon as she thought it, the laces turned a pretty purple. She smiled and pushed open the doors, and went in search of a girl with blue smoke.

"Excuse me? Young lady?"

The voice came out of an official-looking office on Aria's right.

Aria turned. "Me?"

"Yes, you," said a woman at a desk. A little nameplate on the desk said she was Ms. Grover, Head of Student Services. "What do you think you're doing?"

Aria looked around. The woman's tone made it clear she was doing something *wrong*, but she had no idea what.

"You can't just come waltzing in late," explained Ms. Grover. "That's an infraction."

"What's an infraction?" asked Aria.

"Being late."

"No, I mean, what *is* an infraction?"

Ms. Grover straightened her glasses and cleared her throat. "An infraction means a broken rule." She pointed to a poster on the wall. It was covered in sentences that began with *NO. NO* chewing gum. *NO* cell phones. *NO* tardiness . . . "Three infractions equals a detention."

Aria didn't know what a detention meant, either, but decided not to ask. "Sorry," she said. "I didn't know."

Ms. Grover squinted. "What grade are you in?"

"Seventh," said Aria, because she'd been in seventh grade back at Gabby's school. This school seemed very different, but hopefully the numbers stayed the same.

"What's your name?"

"Aria," said Aria.

The woman's gaze narrowed even more. "You don't go here."

Aria frowned. "Yes I do."

"Young lady, there are one hundred and ninety-three girls at Westgate Prep, and I know them all. I don't know you, so you don't go here."

"I'm new," explained Aria, glancing at the laptop on the desk. "You can check," she added. She'd been able to imagine herself onto a class roster at Gabby's school. Surely she could imagine herself into a computer. At least, she *hoped* she could.

Ms. Grover began typing away on the keyboard. "Last name?"

"Blue," said Aria, proud of herself for knowing now that a last name was a second name, not a name you had before the one you have now.

The woman's fingers tapped furiously on the keyboard, and then stopped. "Huh," she said. "There you are."

Aria smiled. The lights in the office brightened slightly. Ms. Grover did not seem to notice.

"You're still late," she said, pushing a stack of pamphlets and papers across the desk toward Aria. "Surely you've already received all of this in the mail, and had time to read through our policies. Normally, we'd have a student ambassador ready to welcome you, but I'm afraid I didn't know you were coming."

"Last minute," said Aria. "I didn't know, either."

"Yes, well, here's your schedule," said Ms. Grover, tapping the paper on top of the stack. "The seventh-grade girls are still at lunch, but it's almost over. Let me see if I can rustle up someone to show you where to go —"

"That's okay," said Aria brightly. "I bet I can find my way."

Ms. Grover hesitated. "Are you sure?"

Aria nodded. She had a student to find, and she wanted to get going. A faint tug in her chest told her the girl was nearby.

"Very well," said Ms. Grover, already turning away. Aria hoisted the papers into her arms and was nearly to the door when the woman said, "And, Miss Blue?"

"Yes, ma'am?"

The woman offered a small, begrudging smile. "Welcome to Westgate."

Aria could barely see over the stack of handouts as she stepped into the hall. The walls of Westgate, she noticed, were cream-colored but pleasant, and sunlight streamed in through the large windows. A potted plant turned ever so slightly greener as Aria walked past.

What a pretty place, thought Aria, readjusting the papers in her arms. She was about to summon a backpack when a voice behind her said, "Hey, you."

Aria turned around to find a student towering over her. The girl was dressed in the same uniform Aria had on, but she wore a silver badge on her shirt pocket that read MONITOR. She was an eighth grader, Aria could tell, not by her height so much as the way she stood, as if she were very important.

"Your shoelaces are purple," said the girl, as if Aria hadn't noticed.

"I know," said Aria. "I almost went with blue but then I —"

"That's a dress code infraction," the girl cut in, crossing her arms. "I'm going to have to write you up."

Aria frowned. "But I already have an infraction for being late."

"Well, now you have two," said the girl. Aria chewed her lip. She had only been at Westgate for ten minutes, and she was one infraction away from a detention, whatever *that* was, and no closer to finding a girl with blue smoke. She wasn't off to a great start.

The monitor wrote down Aria's name on a purple — how ironic — slip of paper. Aria sighed as the monitor set the paper on top of the already-towering stack in Aria's arms, and then frolicked off, probably to find someone else to punish. As soon as the monitor was gone, Aria willed her purple laces back to black, and started off again down the hall.

She was so focused on not dropping the stack of papers in her arms that she didn't see the girl coming toward her, head down. They collided, and the pamphlets and brochures came down in a shower around them.

"Sorry," muttered the girl as she tried to gather up a few of the papers.

"It's all right," started Aria. "I'm —" But the girl was already on her feet again and hurrying away down the hall. Aria stared after her, eyes wide.

The girl's head was bowed, blond hair falling into her face, and the back of her uniform was covered in what looked like ketchup (Aria had discovered what ketchup was only a few days ago). But it wasn't the ketchup that caught her eye, or even the fact that the girl looked like she'd been crying.

It was the blue smoke.

Tendrils of bright blue coiled around the girl's shoulders as she vanished around the corner.

Then Aria realized she wasn't alone in the hall. A girl with straight brown hair had been standing there, watching everything with a small, cruel smile.

"You're new," she said, surveying Aria. It wasn't a question.

Aria nodded. "First day."

"I'm Erica," the girl said, her smile spreading.

"Hi. I'm Aria," Aria answered as nicely as possible, even though something about Erica made her nervous. Maybe it was the way she hadn't helped pick up the papers, only watched. Maybe it was the way she seemed happy about the other girl being upset. "Who was that girl?" Aria asked.

"That," answered Erica, "is Caroline Mason. And my advice," she added, as the bell rang overhead, "is to stay as far away from *her* as possible."

Aria didn't ask why. She didn't have a chance, since Erica was already walking away. But she knew one thing for sure: She had no intention of staying away from Caroline Mason.

Because Caroline Mason was *exactly* who she was looking for.

chapter 3

CAROLINE

"It's going to be the best year ever."

That's what Lily had told Caroline as they rode to Westgate on the first day of seventh grade. That was only three weeks ago, but it felt like years.

Now, Caroline stood in the doorway of the counselor's office, breathless and upset.

She'd kept her tear-filled eyes on the floor all the way to Ms. Opeline's office. Bumping into that redheaded girl in the hallway had made Caroline feel even worse.

"Miss Mason," said Ms. Opeline, looking up from her work. "How can I help you?"

Overhead, the first bell rang.

"I need to borrow a uniform," said Caroline, her face hot.

Ms. Opeline's eyebrows went up. "What's wrong with the one you're wearing?"

Caroline turned around so the counselor could see the disgusting swirl of condiments that ran from the collar of her once-white polo to the hem of her plaid skirt.

"What happened?" asked Ms. Opeline, sounding genuinely concerned.

"It was an accident," answered Caroline. As if Lily and Erica and Whitney hadn't painted the mess on the tray. As if Lily hadn't tricked her into stopping. As if Erica hadn't held the tray up vertically so it would do the most damage.

"Mhmm," said Ms. Opeline, as she went to a closet in the corner of the room and pulled out a fresh uniform. But when Caroline went to take it, Ms. Opeline didn't let go.

"Caroline," she said, "this is the fourth uniform since school started. And it's only September."

"I know," said Caroline slowly. "I'm sorry," she added.

"Don't be sorry," said Ms. Opeline. "Just tell me what's going on."

Caroline's throat tightened. *Lily Pierce is ruining my life*, she wanted to say. But telling Ms. Opeline wouldn't fix it. It would only make things worse, because Ms. Opeline would tell Caroline's parents, and Caroline's parents would tell Lily's parents, and that would only make Lily hate her more, and that was the last thing Caroline wanted, so she said, "Nothing. Everything is fine."

Ms. Opeline sighed. "Okay," she said, letting go of the uniform. Caroline reached the door before Ms. Opeline added, "But if you change your mind, I'm here."

In the bathroom across the hall, Caroline put on the clean uniform. She stuffed the stained clothes into a plastic bag and shoved the plastic bag into her backpack.

"Did you hear what happened to Caroline?" said someone in the hall.

Caroline froze, listening.

"Whatever," said another girl. "She probably deserved it. . . ."

It was like being punched in the stomach. Caroline's throat tightened. She stood there, listening as their chatter died away. She couldn't tell who the girls were, but it didn't matter. Everyone probably felt the way they did. The bell rang, and the thought of going to class, of sitting in a room with those girls — or girls like them — made Caroline wish she were in outer space.

She met her own reflection over the sink. Her blue eyes were red, and her blond hair was flecked with tiny dots of ketchup and mustard. It wasn't supposed to be like this.

"You look out for me, and I'll look out for you. And we'll stick together no matter what."

A few tears began to stream down her face, but she wiped

them away. The second bell rang, and she took several deep breaths, and finished cleaning herself up.

Caroline was only a few minutes late to science.

Science was her favorite subject, or at least it used to be. She didn't have to deal with Lily or Whitney there, but Erica more than made up for their absence.

Erica scrunched up her nose as Caroline walked past.

"Mr. Pincell," she said, raising her hand. "Something smells."

The science teacher sighed. "I don't smell anything, Miss Kline."

"I do," she persisted, looking pointedly at Caroline. "Like someone's been bathing in kitchen trash."

A few other girls giggled. Caroline grimaced and took her seat.

"Focus," said Mr. Pincell. "Today we're going to work in pairs."

Caroline groaned inwardly. There were an odd number of girls in the class, which meant she'd get to sit there, watching everyone else find a partner, until she was the only one left, and Mr. Pincell would ask the class which pair wanted to work with Caroline, and nobody would answer, and —

"Can I be your partner?"

Caroline looked up to see a girl standing over her desk. It was the redhead Caroline had crashed into earlier. It took Caroline a second to process the question because it took her a second to realize someone was speaking to her. Her heart fluttered a little. It was amazing how good it felt, being spoken to.

Westgate Prep was a small school. Certainly small enough that Caroline had memorized the sixty-two students in her grade, and this girl wasn't one of them. She must be new. Which meant the only reason she was talking to Caroline was because no one had told her not to.

Yet.

"I'm Aria," said the girl. "I just started here."

"Caroline."

Aria settled in across the table from her. "So," she said. "Partners?"

Caroline hesitated, then nodded. "Okay."

"Uh," said Aria, scooting her chair closer. "What do partners *do*?"

"Well, right now we're studying crystals," explained Caroline, handing Aria a lump of quartz. "We have to answer the questions on the work sheet."

Aria held the crystal up to the light. "It's beautiful," she said quietly. She then squeezed one eye shut, held the crystal up to her other eye, and considered the class through it.

Aria stopped when she came to Erica's desk and simply stared at her through the crystal. Then she lowered it, and turned toward Caroline.

"That girl keeps making a face at me."

Erica was scowling at Aria so hard it looked like she was trying to burn a hole into her with her eyes. "Erica Kline," said Caroline. "That's pretty much the only face she makes. But also . . ." Caroline looked down at her notebook. "She probably doesn't want you hanging out with me."

Aria looked like she was about to ask why, and Caroline *really* didn't want to try to explain. Except Aria *didn't* ask why. She said, "Oh, I know. She already told me to stay away from you."

Caroline felt her own face drain of color. "Then why did you ask to be my partner?"

Aria smiled and picked up the crystal, gazing through it at the ceiling light. "Because I wanted to."

Caroline stared at her, dumbfounded.

"Ladies," said Mr. Pincell. "Less chat, more work."

Caroline gave him a dazed nod. She and Aria worked in silence for the rest of the class, but Caroline could feel Aria's gaze on her the whole time, and when the bell rang, Aria followed her out.

"Look," said Caroline. "Thanks for being my partner today. But Erica was right. You should probably stay away from me."

Aria tipped her head. "Why's that?"

Caroline sighed. "Because Erica is one of Lily Pierce's minions, and Lily hates me. She told everyone to leave me alone, so if she sees you hanging out with me, it'll make her mad, and trust me, you don't want to make her mad."

"Is that what *you* did?" asked Aria.

Caroline swallowed hard. "Look, I'm trying to do you a favor," she said. Aria's kindness would only make things worse. For *both* of them. "You just got here. You don't know how things work."

"You could tell me."

"I am. I'm telling you that I'm toxic. So unless you want to be Westgate's newest outcast, you should steer clear of me."

"I don't want to."

"Well, I want you to," said Caroline, even though having someone to sit with, to talk to, had made class bearable for the first time in weeks. "So leave me alone." And before Aria could say anything else, Caroline turned and left.

chapter 4

ARIA

Aria watched Caroline walk away from her for the second time that day. She didn't understand what was going on. Who was Lily Pierce? And what had Caroline done to make her mad? Was the whole school really ignoring Caroline just because one girl told them to?

Her thoughts swirled like Caroline's smoke. She looked down at her black laces. She wished they were still purple. She was *sure* she'd be able to think better if they were purple.

She tapped her shoe a few times. And then she got an idea.

Aria ducked into the bathroom. When she entered a stall, she saw a message scribbled on the wall:

Caroline Mason is a waste of space.

Something fluttered in Aria's chest, a sensation she'd never felt before, and it took her a moment to realize what it was: *anger*. She brought her fingertips to the message, and it erased itself.

And then, Aria erased *herself*.

Aria didn't *like* being invisible. It certainly came in handy, but it always left her feeling . . . less than real. Still, if she was going to help Caroline, she needed to understand exactly what was going on, and it seemed like the best way to do that was to watch what Caroline's life was like without Aria in it.

Aria stepped out of the stall, and looked in the mirror, startling a little at the fact that she couldn't see herself in it. And then she went in search of Caroline.

She caught sight of the blue smoke just as Caroline was reaching her last class, art. Aria slipped through the door behind her.

Caroline took her seat, and Aria stood beside her, hoping that even if she couldn't see her there, Caroline might feel a little less alone. Erica sat on the other side of the room next to a girl Aria hadn't seen before. Her backpack said her name was Whitney.

"Good afternoon, class," said the art teacher. He looked exactly like Aria imagined an art teacher would look — cheerful and paint-speckled. His name, she saw on the board, was Mr. Ferris. "It's such a lovely day," he said. "I was thinking . . ."

"That you'll cancel class?" offered a girl.

That started a chorus of "Yeah!" and "Pleeeaasseee," but Mr. Ferris only laughed and held up his hand, and the room quieted again.

"Alas," he said, picking up a notepad. "School policy says no. But I did think we could go outside and draw."

A murmur of approval ran through the room as he began to take roll. "All right," he said when he was done. "The only one we're missing is Lily."

"I'm here, sir."

Caroline stiffened in her seat, and Aria turned to see Lily Pierce standing in the doorway.

"Sorry I'm late," she said, waving a note.

Aria's mouth hung open. Lily had black curls, and pale skin, and a dazzling smile. But it wasn't any of those things that made Aria gape. No, it was something no one else seemed to notice. Something no one else *could* see.

Lily Pierce was surrounded by bright blue smoke.

The art class spread out across the lawn, drawing pads propped on their knees as they sketched with colored pencils. Lily and Erica and Whitney sat in a circle in the center of the lawn, but Caroline sat alone under a tree. She had her head bowed over her paper, and was sketching a fallen leaf, detailing every crack and vein with an orange pencil.

Aria, still invisible, sat beside Caroline, but she couldn't keep her eyes off of Lily. And Lily's smoke. Smoke the same color as Caroline's, a sky blue that matched Aria's bracelet.

It didn't make sense.

Aria had already found the girl marked for her help.

How could there be two?

As she watched Lily smile and laugh and whisper in Erica's ear, a knot formed in Aria's stomach.

The blue smoke marked people who needed her help, but Aria had always assumed that meant people who *deserved* her help. From what she'd heard, Lily Pierce was not a very nice person.

How was Aria supposed to help a girl who was being bullied *and* the girl who was bullying her?

There had to be more to it.

Mr. Ferris paused over Caroline to consider her drawing. "You like science, don't you, Miss Mason?"

Caroline looked up. "Yes, sir. How did you know?"

He gave her a gentle smile, and nodded at her sketch. "You're trying to replicate the leaf, to re-create it on the page, line for line, shadow for shadow. But art is less science," he said, "and more, well, *art*."

"I'm sorry, sir."

"Don't be sorry, Caroline. Just let go. Hold your pencil looser. Don't be afraid to draw a line in the wrong place. And for goodness' sake don't try and erase it if you do. Just make a new line."

Caroline nodded, and Aria found herself nodding, too. She liked this Mr. Ferris, she thought, as a bright red leaf fell out of the tree and floated into her lap. She smiled and held it up to the sunlight. Fall was so full of color. Aria was beginning to think that it was her favorite season. Or at least, her favorite season right now. She hadn't experienced winter or spring yet, so she couldn't be totally sure, but it was definitely her favorite-for-today.

Aria looked up and realized that Caroline was staring at her, eyes wide.

No, not at *her*. At the bright red leaf in her hand. Aria had forgotten that she was invisible, that the leaf must seem like it was hovering in the air, held aloft by magic. Aria quickly let go of the leaf. Caroline watched it float to the ground, then picked it up, and set it on her notepad.

Laughter burst out across the lawn, and Aria turned to see Lily clasping a hand over Erica's mouth. Aria got to her feet and crossed the grass toward them.

When she saw what they were laughing at, she frowned.

Erica had finished drawing her tree and had added a stick-figure version of Caroline, sitting alone beneath it. Three different sets of handwriting had written the words *Loser*, *Freak*, and *Weirdo* in the space around the sketch. Whitney chewed her pencil. Erica smiled smugly. But Lily didn't. Her laughter had trailed off.

Aria studied Lily. Something was wrong. It was in her eyes, in the beats of silence between her laughs. Like she wasn't *really* happy.

Aria sighed and crouched, inches from Lily's face. A ribbon of blue smoke curled between them.

What is it made of? Aria wondered, squinting at the fog. She could understand why Caroline's smoke swirled around her, and could guess the lonely thoughts and feelings it was filled with. But what could Lily need?

The bell rang, and Aria straightened.

"What a loser," said Erica, packing up her supplies. Aria knew she meant Caroline.

"Yeah," echoed Whitney, a bit halfheartedly.

And then Erica added, "I can't believe you two used to be best friends."

Aria froze. *Best friends?* She looked to Lily — and her swirling smoke — as the girl rolled her eyes and said, "I know."

28

But how? How could someone go from being a best friend to being a bully?

Lily and her friends brushed the grass from their skirts and strolled away. Aria turned back in search of Caroline, but she was already gone.

chapter 5

CAROLINE

"Just you today?" asked Caroline's mom after school.

"Just me," mumbled Caroline, climbing into the car.

They went through this every day. At first, Caroline made a dozen different excuses for why there was no more carpool — well, there was, it just didn't involve *her* — but she'd run out of good lies and the energy to tell them convincingly.

"How was school?" asked her mom.

Caroline looked out the window, the lunchroom incident burned into her mind. "It was fine," she lied.

Her mom squinted at her. "Are you wearing a different uniform?"

She looked down at the borrowed clothes. "I spilled food on mine."

"Goodness, Caroline, you've gotten so clumsy. That's the third one this month."

Fourth, thought Caroline. The first time, Lily and Erica had stuffed her clothes in the trash can during gym. The second time, they'd put them in the toilet (Caroline had stood, in the flooded stall, watching the blue-and-green plaid swirl in the toilet water). After that, Caroline made sure to put a lock on her gym locker. For a little while it worked, but that just made them more creative. The third uniform had ended up splattered with mud. And now this.

At least she'd survived art. The last class of the day. And the worst. That's where everything had started.

When they got home, Caroline's mom called upstairs to Megan, Caroline's sister. When there was no answer, she asked Caroline to go check on her.

Megan was stretched across her bed, and she was on the phone. She was always on the phone.

"Mom's looking for you," said Caroline.

Megan waved a hand. "I'll be down soon."

Caroline hesitated. Megan was sixteen and gorgeous and without a doubt the most popular girl at her high school. Caroline couldn't imagine Megan *ever* being bullied.

When Megan saw that she wasn't leaving, she lowered the phone and said, "What do you want?" With her tone, she might as well have said *go away*.

Caroline hesitated. "I . . ."

I need your advice, she wanted to say. *School is a nightmare and I don't know what to do and I'm afraid that if I tell someone like Mom or the counselor or the headmistress it will just make everything worse and I —*

"Well?" pressed Megan, impatiently.

Caroline swallowed. "I wanted to borrow your hairbrush," she said, chickening out.

Megan rolled her eyes, tossed the brush to her, and kicked the door shut with her foot.

Caroline trudged down the hall into the bathroom. She dropped the brush on the counter and dug her ruined uniform out of her backpack, dumping it in the bathroom sink. There was a jewelry box on the counter, and somewhere in the bottom drawer was the half-circle necklace.

We'll stick together no matter what.

She couldn't bring herself to throw the necklace away, but she forced herself to not open the box and take it out.

Instead, she tried to scrub away the stains on her uniform, but they didn't come out, only spread, turning the polo and skirt a sickly orange brown.

Caroline heard a car door slam, and a familiar voice, and her chest tightened. It wasn't bad enough that she had to see Lily every day at school. She was also her next-door neighbor.

Through the bathroom window she could see Lily's black hair as she got out of her mom's car. Lily's smile faltered, and then faded altogether — Caroline knew that Lily hated her strict after-school routine, because that was the kind of thing best friends were supposed to know about each other. She watched Lily hesitate on the porch, as though she didn't want to go inside.

For a second, Caroline didn't hate her. She just felt sorry for her. And then she remembered the ruined clothes sitting in the sink, and she snapped the water off. She left the uniform soaking while she went to her room, and lay down on her bed.

Maybe it was just a bad dream. She wished she could wake up.

Or run away. Some days she thought about running away. Starting a new life.

But Caroline Mason didn't want a new life.

She just wanted her old life back.

. . .

"What about Beth?" Lily pointed across the lunchroom with her fork. It was the first week of seventh grade.

"No," said Erica. "Her sister's in eighth grade here. What about Jessabel?"

Lily shook her head. Caroline knew Lily had a crush on Jessabel's big brother.

"Maybe Caroline should pick," offered Erica.

Caroline frowned. "Why?" she asked. "Why do we need to pick anyone?"

"It's a new year, Car," explained Lily. "We have to send a message. Tell the girls at Westgate that they don't mess with Table Seven."

"But they haven't messed with Table Seven," countered Caroline. "Not yet."

Lily sighed dramatically. "You don't get it."

"No," said Caroline, "I don't."

It wasn't the first time Lily had singled someone out. She used to only go after girls if they did something to make her mad (back in the sixth grade, Lily had been horrible to a girl just because she'd hurt Caroline's feelings). But this time seemed random, and Caroline didn't like it.

"It's preemptive," explained Lily. "We send a message. By the time we're done with whoever we pick, no one will want to take her place. No one will want to get on our bad side. Which means everyone will want to get on our good side. Do you understand now?"

Caroline didn't. But she didn't want to be on Lily's bad side, either, and Lily and Erica were both giving her a you're-with-us-or-against-us look, so she nodded, and tried to ignore the pit in her stomach.

"I know!" said Erica. "What about Whitney Abel?"

"Never heard of her," said Lily.

"She's new," said Erica, pointing across the lunchroom.

A brown-haired girl was sitting at the edge of Table 11, but not talking to the other girls there. She stared down at her food.

"Her clothes don't look new," observed Lily.

"They're not even hers. They're used."

Lily scrunched up her nose. "Gross."

"It's not her fault," Caroline spoke up. "She's here on scholarship."

"How do you know?" challenged Lily.

Caroline shrugged. Her mom was on the school board, and when she found out about Whitney's background — her dad was a single parent and had been laid off after Whitney was accepted to Westgate — she told Caroline to be nice.

"New schools are hard," her mom had said. "And Whitney's had a hard enough time already. Look out for her."

"I think we should leave her alone," Caroline told Lily.

"Overruled," said Lily, daring Caroline to challenge her again.

And Caroline didn't.

The house phone rang, jarring Caroline out of the memory. She imagined picking it up, and hearing Lily's voice saying, "Whatever. This is stupid. Come sit with us tomorrow."

Caroline went downstairs to see who it was. She could hear her mom on the phone in the kitchen, and knew it was just her dad calling from work.

"I noticed that Lily's home," Mrs. Mason said to Caroline when she hung up.

"I know," said Caroline.

"Is everything okay between you two?"

"We're fine."

"She never comes over anymore," pressed her mom. "Are you having a fight?"

A war, thought Caroline. An unfair, uneven, unwinnable war. She knew she should tell her mom what really happened to her uniform. And the ones before. She knew she should tell her — tell *someone* — about the silent treatment, and the other daily torments, and the way it all made her feel horrible and invisible and small. But she couldn't.

Because if she did, it would all be true, and there would be no going back, no making things right. It would be over.

"Caroline?" urged her mom.

"No," she lied, forcing a thin smile. "Everything's fine."

Her mom gave her a long, searching look. "Why don't you go outside? Get some fresh air."

Caroline couldn't say no, not without telling her mom *why* she was avoiding anything that might put her in contact with Lily. So she grabbed a book and trudged out onto the front porch.

chāpter 6

ARIA

Aria had waited until the lawn was empty and the students were gone. Then, when the coast was clear, she flickered back into form, letting out a sigh of relief at being visible again.

She did a quick check to make sure she was all there, but when she got to her charm bracelet, she stopped. Something was different. Something had *changed*. The second ring, the one where her new feather would go once Aria helped Caroline, was now *two* rings, linked together. Two rings and two girls. So it wasn't a mistake. They both needed her help.

She looked down at her shadow. "What do I do?" she asked. "Who do I help first?"

Aria was prone to talking to her shadow because it was always there, and because now and again it answered in its own way.

After all, Aria's shadow wasn't an ordinary shadow, not by any stretch. It took her wherever she needed to go. Wherever she was *supposed* to be. Even if she didn't know where that was, the shadow would.

She tapped her shoe on the ground, and the shadow gave a nervous wiggle, and then turned on like a light. Aria stepped through, and found herself no longer at Westgate, but on the sidewalk of a big, pretty street, in front of two houses. One was green and one was white, and each had a mailbox with a stenciled name. One said MASON and the other said PIERCE.

Caroline Mason and Lily Pierce.

They lived next door to each other. And Aria was standing halfway between them.

She frowned down at her shadow. "Some help you are," she said.

There was a tug in her chest, as if a rope ran between her and the girls, but the girls were in opposite directions, and both were pulling Aria. She needed to make a decision. And judging by her shadow, she'd have to make it on her own.

Okay. Whatever had happened between Lily and Caroline, she reasoned, their problems were obviously intertwined. To help one, she'd have to help the other. But she'd found Caroline first, so she would start with her. After that, she'd figure out what to do about Lily.

Aria smiled.

It felt good to have a plan.

Just then, the front door on the green house banged open. Caroline walked out onto her front porch and slumped into a swing seat with a book.

Aria started toward her. Caroline didn't seem to notice her coming. She was staring up at the sky, like her body was there but her mind was somewhere else.

There were two porch swings, and Aria sank silently into the one across from Caroline. She rocked it back and forth with her toes, hoping to get Caroline's attention. When that failed, she finally said, "Hey."

Caroline jumped and nearly fell out of her swing. "Aria?" she asked, straightening. "What are you doing here?"

Trying to help, thought Aria. But what she said was, "I was walking by and saw you out here, and thought I'd come say hi. And I know you said you didn't want anyone to see me hanging out with you but *A*, we're not at school and *B*, I don't really care what people think."

Caroline glanced next door. "You shouldn't be here."

Aria let the swing come to a stop. "Because of Lily?" she asked.

"Because of Lily," admitted Caroline. "If she sees you, she'll think we're *friends*."

Aria frowned. She'd always thought *friends* was the best thing you could be, but Caroline said it like it was a bad word. "I don't mind."

Caroline shook her head. "If you hang out with me, Lily will make your life miserable."

"I doubt that," said Aria with simple certainty. She'd never been miserable before. "And besides, not everyone's afraid of Lily Pierce."

"Name one girl who isn't."

"Me," said Aria brightly.

Caroline rolled her eyes. "Well, you're new," she said. "You don't know better."

Aria shrugged. "Maybe." She paused, and then, carefully, said, "You two used to be friends, didn't you?"

Caroline cringed. She drew her knees up onto the seat, and wrapped her arms around them. "I don't want to talk about it," she said.

"Okay," said Aria. But she didn't leave. She could tell that Caroline *did want* to talk about it — could see it swirling in her smoke — but she'd figured out that sometimes people just needed a little time.

And sure enough, after a few moments, Caroline broke the silence.

"Before you showed up," she said, "I was thinking about how much I miss summer."

Aria smiled. "I like summer," she said. "Until I got to fall, it was my favorite season."

Caroline looked at her like she was weird. Aria was getting used to that.

"Summer has the best constellations," explained Caroline. "At night I'd lie out on my trampoline and look up at the stars. And during the day, Lily and I would sit by her pool or out here on the swings and drink lemonade and read magazines." She wiped her eyes. "It wasn't supposed to be like this. This year was supposed to be perfect."

Aria shook her head. "Nothing's perfect."

Caroline let out a small, stifled laugh.

"Why is Lily being mean to you?" Aria asked.

"To get back at me, I guess," Caroline said after a moment.

"For what?"

Just then a car pulled up next door and honked. Over Caroline's shoulder Aria saw Lily bob out the front door and down the steps of her house. She'd traded the uniform for jeans and a T-shirt. Erica and Whitney climbed out of the backseat of the car to meet her.

"Let's get out of here," said Lily. She threw a glance at Caroline and added, "Something totally smells."

"Yeah," chimed in Erica. "Someone should take out their *trash*."

Whitney didn't say anything, only stepped aside so Lily could climb in.

Caroline sat motionless. She was gripping the seat so hard her fingers looked white. Aria crossed to her, and sat beside her on the bench, and put her hand on the girl's shoulder.

"Hey," she said softly. "What happened between you two?"

Caroline swallowed hard. "You really want to know?"

Aria nodded. "I really do."

"Okay," said Caroline, looking up. "I'll tell you. It happened in art. . . ."

chapter 7

CAROLINE

It happened in art.

All class, Caroline had a stomachache.

Lily and Erica kept exchanging glances. Caroline knew their plan. And she hated it. It didn't seem right and it didn't seem fair, and her mom's words kept playing in her head.

Whitney's had a hard enough time already. Look out for her.

"We're doing her a favor," Lily had said during lunch.

"Yeah," Erica had chimed in. "After this, she'll have to get herself some new clothes."

Everyone was at their desks, painting different times of day, some dawn and others noon and others dusk. Lily had been painting a cloudy night, so the water in her plastic cup was bluish black. Erica had been painting a sunrise, but she'd used too much paint on purpose to make her water thick and gross, the colors swirling into brown.

Caroline had used as little paint as possible, and hardly rinsed her brush, so her water was still practically clear.

When it was time to clean up, Lily gathered up her cup and Erica's — she passed over Caroline's when she saw how clean it was — and made her way toward Whitney, who was still finishing her sky. She wasn't even looking.

Look out for her.

At the last minute, Caroline stood up, and hurried toward Lily. She only wanted to stop her. It had taken her all class to work up the courage to do it — to think of what she wanted to say, about how this was stupid and wrong and they were better than it — and she reached Lily just in time, and grabbed her shoulder.

But Lily's forward momentum made her stumble backward, away from Whitney and into Caroline. There was a splashing sound, followed by a shriek from Lily, and then the cups tumbled to the linoleum. Everyone turned to look, including Whitney.

When Lily spun on Caroline, the front of her uniform was covered in dirty water.

"What did you do that for?" growled Lily.

45

"I'm sorry," said Caroline, eyes wide. "I was just trying to —"

"Girls, what's going on?" asked Mr. Ferris.

"It was an accident," said Caroline.

"Yeah, sure." Lily wrung out her skirt, brownish water dripping to the floor.

Erica appeared at Lily's shoulder with paper towels. When Caroline tried to help wipe Lily's shirt, Lily shook her off. "It's fine. Get off me."

"You'd better go to Ms. Opeline and borrow a fresh uniform," said the teacher.

Lily scowled at Caroline, then turned on her heel, and stormed out.

"It was an accident," Caroline called after her, but Lily was already gone.

"So that's why Lily turned against you?" Aria asked. Caroline nodded. "Why did she want to spill paint on Whitney?" pressed Aria.

Caroline explained about Lily's plan, to pick a girl and make an example out of her.

"That's horrible," said Aria.

Caroline stared up. "I know. But it worked. Everyone wants to fit in. They want to belong. Be a part of something.

I just wish," she said under her breath. "I wish I could go back."

"What would you do if you could?" challenged Aria. "*Not* stand up for Whitney? You did the *right thing*."

Caroline felt ill. She'd told herself that over and over but it hadn't helped. If it had been the right thing, then why was she being punished for it?

"I thought it would be okay," she said. "I thought *we* would be okay. But everything changed. Lily didn't come over after school that day, and she didn't ride with me the next morning. And when I got to lunch, Whitney was sitting at Table Seven. In my spot. When I went to sit down, all three of them got up and just . . . walked away. Like I wasn't even there." Caroline felt her throat tighten. It was the first time she'd talked about what had happened with *anyone*. She didn't know why she was telling Aria so much. But it felt good to talk. It felt good to have someone to talk *to*, and it was like once she started, she couldn't stop.

"Does Whitney know what you did?" asked Aria.

Caroline shrugged. "I don't think so. And she probably wouldn't listen if I told her. She's exactly where she wants to be. Where *everyone* wants to be. At the popular table."

"Caroline!" called her mom from inside.

She sighed, and stood up. "I've got to go."

Aria hopped off the swing. "Okay. See you at school."

Caroline hesitated. She didn't want to put Aria in Lily's path. Aria claimed she didn't care, but that was only because she didn't know. But it felt so nice to have someone on her side. It made her feel less like a speck of space dust and more like a planet.

Aria was halfway down the stairs when she turned back and said, "Hey."

"Yeah?"

"Thank you."

"For what?" asked Caroline.

"For telling me what happened."

Caroline shrugged. "It doesn't change anything."

Aria smiled, the kind of smile that seemed to brighten the front yard. "It might."

chapter 8

ARIA

Aria got to the other side of the street before she realized that she had nowhere to go.

Gabby had lived in an apartment building with a nice flat roof for Aria to sleep on. But Caroline's roof had points that didn't look very inviting. The house itself looked like it had extra rooms, but Caroline would have to invite Aria in for her to use them. And since she just left, Aria felt kind of weird about going back.

"Where should I go now?" she asked the shadow at her feet. The shadow fidgeted, trying to decide if Aria wanted it to take her somewhere, but she shook her head and said, "Never mind."

She walked up to to a large tree, and sat down at its base to think. Even though the leaves were changing, the weather was warm enough to sleep outside. But Aria didn't want to get caught, and she didn't want to spend the night invisible, not if she had another option. She leaned her head back and took a deep breath.

Then she saw something up in the tree.

It looked like a house.

Aria raised a brow. She had never seen a house in a tree before, but there it was. At first she wondered if *she* had summoned it — it looked like it was held aloft by magic — but then she saw the branches supporting the floor, and the way the old planks were warped by age, and decided it had already been there. (It still seemed magical, though.)

A magical house for a magical girl, thought Aria with a smile.

There was a rope ladder hanging down, and Aria climbed up. The tree house had no door, only an opening in the floor, and a window between two makeshift walls. The wooden boards groaned under her feet, but the structure held steady.

"Hello?" she called out, even though the house was in fact only one room and she could see that it was empty. Still, it seemed polite to ask.

There was a beanbag in one corner, a shelf nailed to one of the rickety walls, and a couple of candy wrappers on the floor, but otherwise the space was bare. The air whistled through the planks of wood. Aria thought the place was perfect.

Her favorite thing about the tree house was the fact that it didn't have a roof. The branches — full of leaves changing color — made a patchy covering, and past them, she could see the sky.

"This will do," Aria said to her shadow.

She summoned up some pillows and sat down, then emptied the contents of the backpack she'd finally conjured onto the floor. She studied the handouts the front office had given her. Handouts on Westgate's history, its reputation, on what to do, and what not to do, and how to dress (though it didn't say anything about purple shoelaces), and how to be a model student. Handouts on clubs, and sports, and a flier for an upcoming dance with Eastgate, which was apparently the boys' school down the road.

Every pamphlet and brochure featured a smiling group of students walking to class or gathered in the halls. But one of the pictures made Aria stop.

Lily Pierce had her arm slung around Caroline Mason's shoulder, their heads together. They were both grinning. The girls didn't just look happy. They looked *inseparable*.

Aria drew her finger lightly over the photograph, and blue lines appeared, like wisps of smoke, wrapping around the two girls. A small purple thumbtack took shape in Aria's palm, and she pinned the pamphlet to the tree house wall.

Her gaze drifted outside to Caroline's house. The girl in the photo hardly resembled the one across the street.

But that was okay.

Aria was here to help.

"Hurry up, Jess, before somebody sees."

"Stop watching me and keep an eye out."

The girls were in the gym, huddled in front of one of the lockers before the bell rang. They'd gotten there early. And so had Aria. She stood invisible, watching as one of them — Jessabel — squeezed packets of ketchup onto a girl's gym clothes. *Caroline's* gym clothes.

"Did Lily tell you to do this?" asked the other girl.

"No," said Jessabel, tearing open another packet. "It's called *initiative*. You have to take it."

Aria frowned. She had spent the morning invisible, wandering the school, listening to the girls in the halls and the classrooms. Getting to know them, and the things they had to say, about life, about school, about Lily, about Caroline. From what she could tell, the students fell into three camps where Caroline Mason was concerned: those who thought she deserved what was happening to her, those who didn't but weren't willing to get involved, and those who might actually talk to Caroline if she ever talked to *them*. Which she apparently hadn't.

Aria had been in the hall when she overhead Jessabel's plan.

"Almost done," said Jessabel now.

"Hurry up," nagged the other girl. "Class is about to start."

Aria watched, conflicted about what to do.

She thought about becoming visible and stopping the girls, or staying invisible and scaring them away. But neither of those things would make them stop tormenting Caroline. So Aria stood and watched and chewed her lip and waited. And when the girls were done, and they dumped the empty packets in the trash and hurried away, Aria flickered back into sight and approached Caroline's locker.

The built-in lock on the door was broken. Aria pressed her hand to the metal, and by the time her fingers fell back to her side, the door was fixed. And so were the clothes inside. She felt rather satisfied with herself, and went to find her own locker, passing Caroline on the way (Caroline kept her head down, and didn't seem to notice her, even though she was definitely visible again).

The locker room started filling up. Aria watched Caroline as she reached her locker and ran her hand over the repaired lock. She watched her turn the little dials and open the door, watched her shoulders slump with relief when she found the clothes inside untouched.

Aria smiled.

And then someone screamed.

It was more of a screech, actually. Coming from Jessabel's locker. Aria crossed her arms. It had seemed like the only fair thing to do. At least until a second later, when Jessabel tore around the corner, clutching her ketchup-splattered gym clothes. She came barreling toward Caroline.

"What did you *do*?" growled Jessabel.

Caroline's eyes widened. "I didn't —"

"What did you do?" Jessabel shoved the ruined gym clothes against Caroline. Aria frowned. It wasn't supposed to happen like this.

"Hey," she said, coming forward. "It wasn't Caroline's fault."

Jessabel spun on Aria. "Was it you?" She charged toward her. "How? How did you —"

"Jessabel," came a voice, and everyone looked up to see Lily standing there in her gym clothes, Erica and Whitney behind her. "What on earth do you think you're doing?" Lily asked, scrunching up her nose.

Jessabel's mouth opened and closed like a fish as she clutched the splattered gym clothes. "I was just . . . trying to . . ."

"To what?" asked Lily with a smirk. "Look ridiculous?" Erica giggled at Lily's shoulder.

Jessabel turned bright red.

Aria stared at Lily, shocked. Was she *standing up* for Caroline?

"Go get cleaned up, before anyone sees you looking like that."

Jessabel huffed and stormed away.

"I think you upset her," said Whitney softly.

"Serves her right," said Lily, running a hand through her hair. "That's what happens when you mix with *trash*." She looked right at Caroline when she said it.

So much for Good Lily, thought Aria. Blue smoke or not, she needed a talking-to. Aria clenched her hands and took a step toward her, but Caroline caught her shoulder.

Don't, she mouthed.

Lily's eyes slid from Caroline to Aria, and hovered there for a long moment. And then Lily turned and left, her minions bobbing in her wake. Caroline's hand fell from Aria's shoulder as she looked down at her polo. It was splattered with ketchup from Jessabel's attack. Her jaw clenched. The blue smoke coiled around her.

"Hey," said Aria gently. "I have an extra shirt. Do you want it?"

After a moment, Caroline nodded reluctantly. "Thanks," she said, looking around. "But don't let anyone see. It will just make it worse."

"Our secret," said Aria, managing a smile, and producing a clean polo from behind her back. And for an instant, Caroline smiled, too. And then the coach whistled, and the smile was gone. The girls got changed and went to join the class.

Westgate's gym was nothing like the last school Aria went to. Here there were tennis courts, and a field, and a massive track, and a fancy swimming pool with three diving boards at different heights.

The rest of the seventh graders were all on the track, some already jogging. Lily and Erica and Whitney stood stretching, and Jessabel sat on the bleachers wearing a spare pair of gym clothes that were obviously three sizes too large. She glared daggers at Aria and Caroline as they made their way to the track.

Caroline said nothing to Aria as they started running,

and Aria stayed a stride or two behind the other girl. But at least Aria knew that Caroline knew she wasn't alone.

For a while, as they jogged, the blue smoke that circled Caroline's shoulders thinned.

Just a little.

But it was a start.

chapter 9

CAROLINE

The noise of the lunchroom washed over Caroline as she clutched her tray. Here she was again. The worst part of her day.

Once again, she felt lost in space. She found herself scanning the room for Aria, but she didn't see her. Girls shouldered past to get to their seats, one knocking into Caroline hard enough that she nearly dropped her lunch tray. She started to make her way toward Table 12, but she couldn't do it, not after yesterday, not with *something smells* and *trash* still echoing in her head.

So Caroline took a deep breath, turned, and left the cafeteria.

Compared to the noisy lunchroom, the hallway was quiet, and through the doors, the courtyard outside was silent, but not in a heavy, lonely way. It was peaceful. She could imagine she was somewhere else. Caroline carried her tray to the steps, and sat down.

She'd just started eating when someone above her cleared his throat, and she looked up to see Mr. Cahill, the assistant headmaster, staring down at her.

"Miss Mason," he said, gesturing to the tray. "What is this?"

"My lunch?" ventured Caroline.

"I can see that," said Mr. Cahill. "What I can't see is why it — and you — are out here instead of in the cafeteria with the rest of your class."

Because I lost my friends, Caroline wanted to say, *and my table, and no one will look at me, let alone talk to me, and yesterday I got hit with a tray of ketchup.*

But she didn't say that. All she said was, "Because it's a nice day."

"That may be," said Mr. Cahill. "But all seventh graders are expected to eat lunch *together*. In the cafeteria. It's been scientifically proven that eating lunch together creates a sense of community. Don't you want a sense of community, Miss Mason?"

Caroline stared up into Mr. Cahill's face. She felt like she was trapped in some kind of sick joke. "Yes, sir, but I can't . . ." She almost said she couldn't go back in there.

"Can't what, Miss Mason?"

Caroline looked down at her tray.

"Did something happen?" he pressed. "Is something wrong?"

Caroline hesitated, then sighed. "No, sir."

"Then unless you want to be issued an infraction, I'm going to have to ask you to go back inside," said Mr. Cahill. "It may not seem like it, but social interaction is an integral part of —"

Just then the doors burst open, and Mr. Cahill and Caroline both turned to see Aria bouncing through, carrying her tray.

"Sorry I'm late!" she said, plopping down beside Caroline.

Caroline felt a rush of relief. "See?" she said to Mr. Cahill. "I'm not eating alone. There's plenty of social interaction happening here."

Mr. Cahill examined both of them. "All right," he said. "But why are you out here and not in the cafeteria?"

"I just started here," Aria said brightly. "Caroline is my student ambassador. The front office told her to show me around, and tell me how things work so I can get caught up as quickly as possible. Caroline thought it would be easiest for us to meet during lunch so we could talk. No time to waste. This is a hard school, and every moment you're not ahead, you're falling behind."

It sounded like a line from one of Westgate's brochures.

"Besides, it's awfully loud in the lunch room," continued Aria. "And a bit overwhelming. So Caroline agreed to meet me out here where it was calmer."

Mr. Cahill turned to Caroline. "Is that true, Miss Mason?"

Caroline nodded. "Yes, sir."

Mr. Cahill gave a small huff. "All right, but today only, ladies. Tomorrow it's back to the lunch room, understand?"

"Sure thing," said Aria.

As soon as he was gone, Aria slumped back against a stone pillar. "He's pretty stern."

"You didn't have to cover for me," said Caroline, picking at her food.

Aria shrugged. "I don't mind. You *could* be my student ambassador. They never gave me one yesterday. And the lunch room *is* really noisy."

Caroline nodded, and went back to poking her food. When she snuck a glance at Aria's tray, she saw that it was covered in fruit. Apple, banana, orange, grapes, even a kiwi.

"I'm trying to decide which one is my favorite," said Aria, as if that explained everything. "I think it's important to know. And I thought it would be easier if I just focused on one food group at a time."

Caroline laughed. Not a loud laugh, and not a very strong one, but the sound of it still surprised her. And for a second, everything felt a little lighter. "I guess it does make sense," she said. "In a weird kind of way."

Aria beamed, and picked up her apple. "So," she said, biting into it, "what *are* you doing out here?"

Caroline's spirits sank again. "I needed some fresh air."

Aria tilted her head back. "It *is* hard to sit inside when the weather's this nice." She looked back at Caroline. "So it had nothing to do with Lily?"

Caroline frowned. "I didn't want to sit alone."

"There's more than one table in the cafeteria. Why not sit at one of the others?"

Caroline shook her head. "Even if I sat with someone else," she explained, "I'd still be sitting alone." Aria didn't understand what it was like. To be hated. To be ignored. Up until this year, Caroline hadn't known how it felt, either. But now she did, and with that knowledge came a certainty that the other girls at Westgate would never be her friends.

"Well," said Aria, looking up past the buildings. "This is better than a lunch table. Even if it's just for today."

Caroline followed her gaze. The sky was streaked with clouds. Back when she and Lily were BFFs, they'd pick out shapes and make up stories about them. Caroline saw pirate ships and mountains and wolves, but Lily always said she saw castles. Sometimes the castles had princesses trapped inside, high up in towers and guarded by dragons.

But these clouds weren't the kind for finding shapes. They were long and thin.

"Those are my favorite," Caroline said, pointing at them. "People usually like cumulus clouds, those big, puffy ones, but these are stratus. They look like someone drew them with a piece of chalk, but they make the best sunsets."

"Sorry," added Caroline when Aria didn't answer. "I know that's nerdy."

"Don't be sorry," said Aria. "It's awesome. You're really smart," she added. She didn't say it like it was a bad thing. "Why would I tease you for that?"

Caroline sighed. "I don't know."

"Hey, Lily?"
"Yeah, Car?"

"Want to know something cool?"

It was a summer night, a week before the start of seventh grade, and they were stretched out on the trampoline in Caroline's backyard.

Lily propped her head on her elbow. "Sure."

Caroline gazed up at the stars. "Light takes a really long time to travel through space, so when we look at the night sky, we're actually looking at a past version of it."

The universe was so amazing, and vast, and full of cool facts and secrets, and the thought of all the things she knew and didn't know and wanted to know made Caroline smile.

But Lily only snorted, and slumped back down. "You sound like such a nerd," she said. Caroline deflated. "Promise me you're not going to go around sounding off random fact bites when school starts."

Caroline sighed. "I promise."

"Hey now, don't pout," said Lily. "I'm only looking out for you."

The first bell rang, a warning that lunch would be over in five minutes.

Caroline blinked, dragging herself out of the memory. Aria had collected several brightly colored leaves and was twirling them between her fingers. *She's a little strange*, Caroline thought. But she liked how Aria didn't seem to hide her strangeness. Caroline envied that.

She got to her feet with her tray, but the thought of returning to the cafeteria made her feel sick.

"Here," said Aria, holding out her hand. "I'll take it back for you."

"Are you sure?" asked Caroline.

"It's no big deal," she said. "I'll see you in science."

"Hey," Caroline called after her.

"Yeah?"

Caroline hesitated. She didn't want to incur Lily's wrath. But she was tired of having no orbit. "If we pair up again," she said, "do you want to be my partner?"

To her relief, Aria broke into a grin. "Sure!"

She ducked inside, and Caroline stood there, feeling something like hope for the first time in ages.

chapter 10

ARIA

Aria made her way back to the cafeteria without spilling anything, which was quite a feat considering there were still a lot of loose grapes (they were her least favorite) as well as a half-eaten apple rolling around on her plate. She was returning the trays to their proper shelves when a voice behind her said, "There you are."

Aria turned to find Lily, Erica, and Whitney standing side by side, forming a wall of plaid skirts and white polos. Lily was actually a half step in front of the other two girls. Not far enough to seem apart, just far enough to show she was the one in charge. Her blue smoke swirled around her even as she smiled.

"It's Ari, isn't it?"

"Aria," she corrected. "Aria Blue."

"You're new here, aren't you?" Lily asked with a sweet smile.

Aria nodded. "I started yesterday."

"Ah," said Lily, tilting her head. "Well, that explains it."

"Explains what?" asked Aria.

Lily ignored the question. "See, Erica?" she said to the girl on her right. "I told you there was a perfectly good reason. I bet nobody told her."

"Told me what?" asked Aria.

Lily turned her attention back to her. "You've been hanging out with Caroline Mason." It wasn't a question.

Aria stood up straighter. "Yeah. I have."

"You're not supposed to do that," cut in Erica.

Lily held up her hand and gave an exasperated sigh.

"You're new at Westgate, so maybe you didn't get the memo, but Caroline Mason does not exist."

"Of course she does," said Aria.

Lily's smile disappeared. "No. She doesn't. You don't talk to her. You don't hang out with her. You definitely don't become her friend. Caroline Mason is *off-limits*."

"Why?" challenged Aria.

"Because I said so," said Lily. And then she smiled again. "Starting at a new school is hard, Ari. You want to make friends. You want to fit in. I get it. But you want to make the *right* friends. You don't need to waste your time on Caroline."

"I —"

"Why don't you come sit with us at lunch tomorrow?" offered Lily sweetly. "Table Seven. We'll help you settle in." She closed the last of the gap between them. "You get to choose the kind of life you have here at Westgate. I can make it awesome, or I can make it awful. But it's your choice, so make the right one."

The bell rang overhead, and Lily flashed her brightest, whitest smile. "Erica, you and Ari have science now, right? Why don't you walk to class together?"

Aria felt dazed from her encounter with Lily. Looking at Lily Pierce was like looking at two images of somebody at the same time, overlapping so that both of them were blurry. There was Lily, who smiled and bossed and acted superior. And there was Lily's smoke, which was full of sadness and frustration and worry, things she kept beneath the surface, behind that smile.

Aria tried to make sense of it as she followed Erica to

class. Erica wasn't surrounded by any smoke. She seemed to wear her meanness on her sleeve.

Erica didn't say a word to Aria the whole way, and then, just before they reached the door, she looped her arm through Aria's, and flashed her a sharp grin. As they went inside, Erica suddenly laughed, as if Aria had said something funny, even though she hadn't said anything at all.

"Girls," warned Mr. Pincell. "You're late."

"Sorry," said Erica cheerfully, letting go of Aria's arm. "I was just showing Aria around."

Aria glanced at Caroline, who looked confused. Aria wished she could explain, but she knew she had to take her seat. She hoped they'd have to pair up, but it turned out not to be a partner day.

As class started, Erica passed Aria a note.

What's your fave color?

Aria wasn't sure why the girl was asking — Erica didn't strike her as the type to care. *Blue*, she wrote. Then she added *red* below it, before finally writing *purple* underneath, because she couldn't decide. She slid the note back to Erica, and went back to listening to Mr. Pincell. But only a few minutes later, another piece of folded paper found its way onto her desk.

When did you move here?

Aria wrote down *yesterday* and sent the paper back.

The third time the paper came to Aria, it didn't have a question on it. Instead it said, *Caroline Mason isn't worth your time.*

Aria frowned, and looked over at Caroline's desk. She was surprised to see Caroline staring at her, or rather, at the paper in her hand. The blue smoke swirled around Caroline's shoulders and Aria realized what it must look like, what Erica was *making* it look like. Showing up late to class, the hooked arms, the passed notes . . . it looked like they were friends.

Aria didn't send Erica's note back. Instead, she crumpled it up and shoved it in the back of her notebook, and started writing one to Caroline.

It's not what it looks like.

Caroline didn't write back, so Aria sent another.

It's <u>REALLY</u> not what it looks like.

Still nothing. Caroline kept her eyes on the board. Aria sighed, and tried one last time. But instead of writing a note, she drew a picture. Of a monster with rows of teeth and squinty eyes and lots of hair. The monster was dressed in a plaid skirt.

Under it she wrote *Erica Kline.*

She was about to pass it to Caroline when she stopped herself. What would happen if Mr. Pincell caught her and took the drawing? What would happen if Erica saw it? Aria had only been trying to make Caroline smile. It hadn't even occurred to her that she was making fun of someone else at the same time. Putting one person down to lift someone else up. That was something bullies did.

Aria wasn't a bully.

She crumpled the paper and shoved it into her backpack.

A few moments later, Caroline finally passed her a note. *I wish it was a partner day.*

Aria wrote back, *Me too.*

chapter 11

CAROLINE

"So," said Mrs. Mason at dinner that night. "How was school?"

It had become Caroline's most dreaded question. But for the first time in a long time, the true answer wasn't *horrible*. It was still bad. Still full of stress and worry and nausea. But not horrible. Thanks to Aria.

"It was okay," she said. "There's a new girl. I'm sort of . . . showing her around." Even though Aria didn't seem to need much showing around, now that Caroline thought about it.

Her mom brightened. "That's really nice of you. Starting at a new school —"

"— is hard, I know." It was the same lecture her mom had given her about Whitney Abel. "It's not a big deal."

"It is," said her mom. "And I'm proud of you, Car." She turned to Caroline's dad. "Isn't that great, honey?" Mr.

72

Mason, who'd been reading a book at the table, mumbled something that sounded like *yes*. Across from him, Megan was texting. Her mom sighed, and turned back to Caroline. "Well, *I* think it's great."

Caroline asked to be excused, then got up and put her plate in the sink. She headed for the back door.

"Where are you off to?" asked her mom.

"Just out back," she said.

"Car —"

"Let her go," Caroline's dad finally joined in. "A little stargazing never hurt anyone."

"I'm just worried about her. . . ." she heard her mom say before the door swung shut.

Out in the yard, Caroline climbed up onto the trampoline. It wasn't full dark yet, so there were no stars, but she stared up at the clouds. They *had* made a really good sunset, just like she knew they would.

Her mind wandered, as it always did, back to summer, when everything was perfect. When she didn't dread waking up. When the hardest question was what to wear to the mall, and the worst thing she had to deal with was the occasional jab from Erica, who only had an attitude because she was jealous that Lily liked Caroline best.

Lily had an amazing heated pool with a slide and a sloped

shallow end like a beach where they could sit, and during the summer they would gather there, with cool, clear water washing up over their legs while they talked.

If Caroline tried hard enough, she could almost hear the sounds of summer, the splash of a pool party, the echoes of laughter. . . .

And then she opened her eyes and realized the sounds weren't part of her memory at all. They were coming from next door. Chatter and soda cans and the voices of Erica and Whitney, and then Lily's voice, calling a meeting to order. Lily loved holding meetings.

A wave of nausea rolled over Caroline as she wondered if the meeting was about *her*.

It was still warm out, but Caroline shivered. She could hear Erica's sharp laugh, and it made her think about her walking into science, arm in arm with Aria. Why was Aria hanging out with her? Yes, Aria had tried to explain in her note, but Caroline still wasn't sure. And she wanted to know, because she really liked Aria. The new girl was starting to feel almost like a friend, but . . .

And then a horrible thought crept into Caroline's head: What if it was too good to be true?

She closed her eyes, and took a deep breath, and pushed

the idea away. And then she heard a voice, much closer than the ones next door, say, "Can I come up?"

Caroline blinked to find Aria resting her elbows on the rim of the trampoline.

"Aria?" she asked, sitting up. "What are you doing here?"

"Your mom let me in," she said, pointing to the house. "So, can I join you?"

Caroline nodded, and Aria hopped up onto the platform and nearly fell over. As she fought to keep her balance, Caroline chuckled. "Haven't you ever been on one of these before?"

Aria shook her head and sank down beside her, sitting cross-legged. The force bounced Caroline up and down a little. "It's like Jell-O," said Aria, poking the elastic floor.

"It's a trampoline," said Caroline. "Here, do what I do."

Caroline stretched out, her head in the center of the trampoline, her feet to the edges. Aria did the same thing, going the other way, and they lay there in the almost-dark as stars began to show up overhead.

There was something about the stars — and about Aria — that made Caroline feel safe.

"Three years," she said absently. "That's how long Lily and I have been best friends. Lily wasn't always so . . . the way she is now." Caroline couldn't believe she was making excuses for her.

"When did she change?" asked Aria.

Caroline squinted, making the starlight blur. "When we started sixth grade at Westgate. Maybe it's because of her mom, but Lily decided that she wanted to be queen bee. She said she *had* to be. And she said she wanted me to be with her. No matter what happened — no matter how she was around other people, or *to* other people — she was always on my side. And I was always on hers." Caroline thought of all the things she'd done for Lily. "It got worse when she met Erica. Lily treated her like a pet project. Erica and I never got along great, but the three of us were fine. Everything was fine. Until now."

Aria drew up her knees. She was still wearing her school uniform, but Caroline noticed that her shoelaces were bright pink. "So," said Aria, "what are we going to do?"

"About what?" asked Caroline.

"About you. About this."

"It's not your problem."

"But I'm here to . . ." Aria trailed off. "I want to help," she said.

"How?" asked Caroline.

"We can stand up to her."

Caroline slumped back against the trampoline. "No," she said. "We can't."

"Yes we can," pressed Aria. "And I bet if we do, others will, too."

Aria obviously knew nothing about Westgate. Silence fell over them, and Caroline realized how much she hated being surrounded by it every day. And how nice it was to have Aria there with her, making the quiet feel warm instead of cold. And since the other girl clearly wasn't going to stay out of things — even if Caroline asked her — she broke the silence and said, "Hey, Aria?"

"Yeah, Caroline?"

"Do you want to ride to school together?"

And even though she wasn't looking at her, Caroline could *feel* Aria smile.

"Yeah," Aria said, tucking her hands behind her head. "I'd love that."

chapter 12

ARIA

Aria paced back and forth on Caroline's front path the next morning, waiting for her to come out. Caroline had offered to pick her up, but Aria had insisted on meeting her instead, since she didn't really know how to explain that she lived in a tree.

It was a pretty Wednesday, all blue sky and cool breeze, and Aria had a good feeling about the day. Now that Caroline was finally opening up, she could help her move forward. Stand up to Lily and her old group. Make a new start.

Aria glanced beyond the picket fence to the house next door.

She still didn't know what to do about *Lily*.

As if on cue, the front door swung open, and Lily Pierce strode out, her black curls pulled back by a green headband. Aria squinted at the girl's blue smoke, as if by looking hard

78

enough, she could see what Lily needed. How she was supposed to help.

Lily saw Aria standing there, and smiled.

It was a contagious kind of smile, and Aria found herself smiling back. There had to be more to her than met the eye. More than meanness and control. After all, Lily and Caroline had been friends for years.

Lily wasn't always so . . . the way she is now. That's what Caroline had said. The new Lily was the problem. Maybe there was some of the old Lily left in there somewhere. Aria just needed to find it.

Lily walked over, and rested her elbows on the fence.

"Hi, Ari," she said cheerfully. "Whatcha doing here?"

"Waiting for my ride," Aria replied.

Lily gave her a pitying sigh. "Why don't you ride to school with us? Erica and Whitney should be here any second."

"That's okay," said Aria. "I'm going with Caroline."

Lily frowned. "I thought we talked about this," she said coolly.

Aria looked into Lily's eyes. "You used to be best friends, didn't you? What happened?" she asked, even though she already knew. She wanted to hear Lily's side.

Lily tossed her hair. "I outgrew her," she said. "The truth

is, I only stayed friends with her so long because I felt sorry for her."

But her blue smoke tightened around her shoulders when she said it.

"You know, Lily," said Aria simply. "I don't believe you. I think you still care. I think you miss her."

For an instant, Lily's smile faltered. And then it was back, tighter than before. She leaned closer. "Look, I'm trying to help you. Ride to school with us. Sit with us. You'll be one of the most popular girls at Westgate. I'm giving you a chance to be someone."

"I'm already someone," said Aria softly, but Lily either didn't hear, or didn't listen.

"A lot of girls would kill to be friends with me," she said, pursing her lips. "You should accept my offer."

Aria leaned in. "Or what?" she asked, truly curious.

Lily's smile fell. "Or stay with Caroline, and be a total loser." She pulled away. "It's simple. You can be somebody. Or you can be nobody. It's your choice."

Aria's brow crinkled. "Are those my only two options?"

Just then, someone honked a horn. Lily pulled back from the fence and waved to the car, where Erica and Whitney were waiting inside.

"Well?" Lily asked Aria. "Are you coming or not?"

Aria looked from Erica and Whitney in the car to Lily at the fence, and then up at Caroline's house. She shook her head. "Thanks for the offer," she said, "but I'll stay."

Lily rolled her eyes. "Fine," she muttered, turning to go.

"Hey, Lily," said Aria.

"What?" she snapped.

"It doesn't have to be like this," said Aria. "You don't have to be like this."

Lily sneered. "You don't know anything. You're just like Caroline. A *nobody*."

She marched off toward the car, and Aria sighed. "What am I going to do about her?" she asked her shadow, but her shadow didn't seem to have a clue.

A second later, Caroline came storming out of her own house.

"Oh, hey!" said Aria, trying to recover. "You ready to go?"

But Caroline didn't even say good morning, just got into the car and shut her door. Caroline's mom appeared a second later.

"Someone's in a mood," said her mother in a singsong way.

"Is everything okay?" asked Aria.

"I'm not sure," said Caroline's mom as they walked toward the car. "She's been so up and down lately, I can't keep track." Aria had met Mrs. Mason last night, when she'd come by to see Caroline. Caroline's mom seemed very nice, but Aria could tell she didn't know about her daughter's predicament.

Now Aria climbed in beside Caroline. She'd never been in a car before. There were lots of buttons, but she resisted the urge to push them. Instead, she leaned in toward Caroline.

"What's wrong?" she whispered. Caroline didn't answer. Her smoke swirled furiously around her. Aria's spirits fell. She had really thought this was going to be a *good* day.

"Seat belts," instructed Caroline's mom, tapping the strap across her lap. Aria found the pieces, and fit them together. "So, *Aria*," she added once they were on the road, "that's a pretty name."

"Thank you," said Aria, glancing over at Caroline. Caroline didn't look back.

"And you just moved in down the road?"

"Yes, ma'am."

"Which house?"

Aria couldn't exactly say the *tree* house, so she said the blue one, because the tree house was indeed painted blue.

"The blue one?" said Caroline's mom. "I can't think of any blue one besides the one Mrs. Hinkle lives in, and *she* certainly didn't move away. . . ."

"Um," said Aria, who didn't like lying and wasn't very good at it. "It's actually more of a green house. Blue green."

"Ah," said Caroline's mom. "Well, we'll have to have your family over for dinner sometime. Do you have any siblings?"

"No," said Aria. "Just me."

"I bet Caroline *wishes* she were an only child, don't you, sweetheart?"

Caroline made a sound that could either have been a *yes* or a *no*.

"So, Aria, how are you liking Westgate? It's an amazing school. Fabulous athletic program. Do you play sports? Caroline here was thinking about joining the swim team. She's an excellent swimmer . . ."

Caroline's mom went on like that for the rest of the ride to school, filling the car with chatter. Which was fine because Caroline remained silent. When the car stopped, she unfastened her seat belt and stormed out without saying good-bye to her mom.

Or waiting for Aria.

By the time Aria got out of the car, Caroline was halfway to the front doors.

"Hey," she called, jogging after her. "Hey, Caroline, wait up!"

chapter 13

CAROLINE

Caroline had seen *everything*.

She'd been getting ready for school, and for the first time she wasn't dreading it. Because she wasn't going alone. She'd be with Aria. The thought made her feel light. And then, as she was pulling on her shoes, she looked out her bedroom window at the front yard below, and she saw them.

Lily Pierce leaning across the fence talking to Aria. Lily was smiling, not her mean smile but her nice one, the one she only used around her friends. It was like a punch in the stomach. And then Aria leaned in as Lily whispered something in her ear. Lily looked up when she said it. At the bedroom window on the second floor.

At Caroline.

And Caroline had realized in that moment what was happening.

What *must* be happening.

It was all some kind of sick game.

Caroline reached her locker, grabbed her books, and slammed it shut. She hurried down the hall, past the other students, wiping away stray tears.

"Caroline?" came Aria's voice behind her, but she kept walking.

She should have known. The more she thought about it, the more it made sense. The reason Aria was being so nice. The reason she was so intent on spending time with her. The reason she wasn't afraid of making Lily mad.

It was a setup.

Lily was so determined to make her life a nightmare that she'd talked the new girl into pretending to be friends with Caroline. And then what? One day, Lily would snap her fingers, and it would all go away.

"Caroline!" called Aria, catching up.

"Just stay away from me." Caroline stormed into the stairwell.

"What did I do?" asked Aria, following.

Caroline reached the top of the stairs and started toward a door, but Aria blocked her way. "Talk to me," she said, breathless. "Please. I don't understand —"

"I saw you talking to Lily."

"So?" said Aria, looking confused. "She showed up while I was waiting for you."

Caroline shook her head. "I've been trying to figure it out."

"Figure what out?"

"You. Why you're so determined to hang out with me. And I get it now, so just admit it."

Aria stared at her, eyes wide. "Admit what?" she asked, tugging on her blue charm bracelet.

Caroline's chest tightened. "You don't even want to be my friend, do you?"

Aria's eyebrows went up. "Of course I do! Caroline, why would I hang out with you if I didn't want to?"

"Because Lily put you up to this," said Caroline, backing away. "To trick me. She —"

"Lily didn't put me up to anything," insisted Aria. "I promise. I'm —"

"I don't believe you," said Caroline, taking another step back. "This is what you and Erica were writing notes about in class. . . ."

"It's not like that. I'm here to help you."

"You probably were even at their pool party last night —"

"Caroline —"

"So you could all figure out the best moment when you'd switch from being my friend to my enemy and —"

"*Caroline,*" said Aria, exasperated. "You're wrong. I'm not their friend, and I'm not your enemy. I'm your —"

Caroline took another step back. Only there wasn't any more landing, only concrete steps, and Caroline lost her balance, and slipped, and started to fall.

And then something happened.

Something *impossible*.

Aria, who was all the way at the other side of the landing, too far away to catch her, *disappeared*. The ground beneath her flashed a brilliant white, and swallowed her up, and an instant later it spit her out. Now she was right next to Caroline, and her hand closed around Caroline's wrist, catching her before she could fall.

Caroline's heart raced as she stared at Aria, wondering if she was going crazy.

"I've been trying to tell you," said Aria, pulling Caroline safely back onto the landing. "I'm not their friend. And I'm not your enemy. I'm your guardian angel."

chapter 14

ARIA

It wasn't exactly how Aria had planned on telling Caroline.

In fact, Aria hadn't *planned* on telling her at all. Or at least, she hadn't thought that far ahead.

But when Caroline had taken that step back, and Aria had used her shadow to catch her, well —

It was kind of hard *not* to tell Caroline after that.

The words had tumbled out, and now that they were there, Aria couldn't take them back.

Caroline's stare was perfectly blank.

Disbelief. Aria could handle that. She braced herself for the onslaught of questions, but the first thing Caroline said, very quietly, was, "So Lily *didn't* put you up to it?"

Aria broke into a smile. "No."

Caroline's brow furrowed as the rest of her questions caught up. "How can you be a guardian angel?" she asked.

"I just am," said Aria. "It's all I've ever been."

"But you don't *look* like a guardian angel. And what do you even *mean*, guardian angel? Like, *literal* guardian angel? Like wings and miracles and halos guardian angel?"

Aria scratched her head. "Um, well, I'm still earning my wings, and I can't really do miracles. . . ."

"What about the thing you just did with the light?" challenged Caroline. "What was that?"

Aria looked down at her shadow and shook her head. "I'm not really sure," she admitted. She'd never moved like that before. She guessed she hadn't *needed* to before. The shadow had appeared when she needed to reach Caroline. "I guess that was a kind of miracle! But I don't have a halo." She patted on top of her hair to be sure.

Caroline kept shaking her head. "You can't expect me to believe this."

"You don't have to," said Aria. "But it doesn't change the fact that it's true. I'm here to —"

The door at the top of the stairs burst open and a handful of sixth graders stormed past them. Caroline and Lily waited for the girls to disappear. And then Caroline's eyes grew larger and she let out a surprised sound.

"Wait. *You're* the one who put the ketchup on Jessabel's gym clothes," she said.

"Technically," said Aria, "Jessabel put the ketchup on *your* gym clothes. I just put your gym clothes in *Jessabel's* locker."

Caroline cracked a smile. "Magic," she whispered, still looking at Aria in wonder. "So have you been, like . . . watching me my whole life?"

Aria shook her head. "I only show up when someone needs my help."

Caroline nodded, her smile fading. "I guess I could use some," she said quietly. Aria could tell it was a hard thing to admit. "So if Lily really *didn't* put you up to this —"

"She *didn't*," insisted Aria.

"Then why were you talking to her?"

Aria sighed, and leaned back against the banister. "She was trying to get me to ditch you. So was Erica. They told me I should sit with them. Hang out with them." She straightened. "But *I stood up to her.* I told her *no.* That I'd rather hang out with you."

Caroline sighed. "Thanks, but you shouldn't have done that. Now Lily is going to make things awful for *you.*"

Aria grabbed Caroline's hand and squeezed. "I'm not too worried."

Caroline looked at Aria, dazed. "Hang on. You didn't tell Lily you were a guardian angel, did you?"

Aria smiled. "No way. That should be our secret for now."

· · ·

Unfortunately, it turned out that Caroline was right about Lily – she *was* going to make things awful. For both of them.

It was gym, and Aria and Caroline were still in the locker room, after everyone else had gone to their next class. They were searching for their uniforms, both of which had mysteriously gone missing from their lockers. There was no doubt it was Lily's handiwork.

"We're going to be late!" cried Caroline.

"Can't we just go to class in these?" asked Aria, gesturing down to her gym clothes. "We can explain what happened."

"No, we can't," said Caroline. "And I can't go back to Ms. Opeline." Aria didn't know who Ms. Opeline was, but Caroline seemed adamant. "Besides, the uniforms have to be here somewhere."

Aria had already offered to summon two new uniforms into existence, but Caroline had refused. "I'm sick of losing my own," she'd said. "I want it back." Caroline still didn't seem *entirely* convinced that Aria was an angel. She kept shooting glances at her as if she was trying to catch sight of Aria's non-existent halo.

"How did she even get into our lockers?" wondered Aria aloud as she stood on a bench.

Caroline sighed and shut the last of the unassigned lockers at the end of the aisle.

"Duct tape," she said. "She put duct tape on the inside of the locks so they wouldn't close all the way."

"Huh," said Aria, hopping down. "That's kind of clever."

"Come on, let's check outside." Caroline pushed the doors open. She scanned the field, the flagpole, the track, the pool . . . and then she looked up.

"Oh no," she said.

"Well at least we found them," said Aria, following Caroline's gaze.

Two plaid skirts rippled in the breeze. Four polo sleeves fluttered. Aria and Caroline's uniforms were hanging from the tallest diving board.

Caroline looked like she might cry. "I'm afraid of heights," she murmured. "Lily knows that. I told her when we first met," she added. "She tried to make me bounce too high on the trampoline, and I freaked out, and she teased me about it, about having a trampoline and not wanting to use it. And I told her that I liked to lie down on it, and watch the sky, and after that, Lily insisted we rename the trampoline an observatory, and said it couldn't be used for jumping, only cloud watching and stargazing." Caroline's hands curled into fists. "She knows I'm afraid of heights, Aria. She did this on purpose."

"It's okay," said Aria softly. "I'm not scared of heights. I'll go get them."

Caroline looked at her, eyes wide. "Are you sure?"

"I'm your guardian angel," said Aria, flashing her a smile. "It's the least I can do."

There was a metal fence around the pool with a gate, but thankfully it wasn't locked. Aria pushed it open, walked across the concrete rim of the pool to the ladder, and looked up at the uniforms draped across the highest diving board.

The highest diving board was, as the name suggested, very high off the ground.

Aria *wasn't* afraid of heights, but the thin ladder and the narrow board did make her a *little* nervous. It didn't help that the whole structure groaned as she started to climb. Nor did it help that Aria knew she couldn't fly (she had tried once, and it hadn't gone very well).

But Caroline was clearly upset, and Aria could help. And in truth, she kind of wanted to impress Caroline. So up she went.

When Aria finally reached the top and stepped out onto the board, she looked down. She could see the crisp blue water glittering in the sunlight, and Caroline standing there, looking much smaller than Aria expected. Caroline shielded her eyes against the sun and Aria waved. The board wobbled faintly under her feet.

"Be careful!" Caroline called up.

And Aria was. But as she started to gather up the uniforms, one of the sleeves got caught on the corner of the diving board. She tugged it free, and it came loose faster than she thought it would.

"Uh-oh," said Aria as she stumbled back . . .

And over the side of the board . . .

And down toward the pool.

She'd fallen once before, from a much higher place (the top of a seven-story apartment building), and her shadow had caught her. But this wasn't *that* high and the world beneath was water instead of sidewalk, so Aria wasn't terribly surprised when she just kept falling toward the water, and hit it with a giant splash that stung her skin and knocked the air out of her lungs.

Aria had never been underwater before.

Overhead, she could see the uniforms floating.

There was only one problem. A problem Aria hadn't thought of until she was there in the cool blue pool, looking up.

She didn't know how to swim.

chapter 15

CAROLINE

Caroline had been standing at the edge of the pool, looking up at Aria, trying to decide if she believed the girl was *actually* a guardian angel.

She had never really believed in things like magic or angels. She believed in science, in the stars in the sky, and the world she could see with her own eyes. But she could see Aria, too, so she knew she was real, and she'd seen her disappear and reappear with her own eyes, even if she didn't understand how.

And really, when she thought about it, the universe was so big that even scientists didn't understand *everything* about it. In fact, one of her favorite things about outer space was that, no matter how much they found, no matter how much they thought they knew, there were more still things to be discovered. More mysteries to be solved.

Maybe Aria was one of those mysteries.

Maybe . . .

Caroline's thoughts were interrupted by a sound — a voice saying "uh-oh" — and she looked up just in time to see a small redheaded shape plummeting down toward the pool.

Aria landed with a splash, followed a second later by the uniforms, which floated down and settled on top of the water. Caroline groaned and waited for Aria to bob back to the surface.

But Aria didn't come up.

Caroline could *see* her there, under the water, and it didn't occur to her at first that Aria might need help, because if she really was a guardian angel, surely she didn't need saving.

And then Caroline realized she didn't know anything about guardian angels, because she'd never met one before, let alone had her own, and it appeared that *this* guardian angel or girl or whatever she was couldn't swim.

And Caroline could.

She pulled off her shoes and socks, took a deep breath, and dove into the water, the way she had a hundred times at Lily's pool. She swam out to the deep end, and then down until she reached Aria.

Aria didn't seem very concerned — she was just kind of hovering there, dragging her arms and legs back and forth —

and when she saw Caroline, she actually *smiled*. And then she tried to say something, and a stream of bubbles came spilling out, followed by a lot of gasping and coughing. Caroline hooked her hands under Aria's arms and dragged her toward the surface, and a couple seconds later they both broke through the water.

Caroline hauled a spluttering Aria up beside her. She grabbed the uniforms floating on the surface and dragged two sets of clothes and one maybe-guardian-angel to the edge of the pool.

"Why didn't you come up for air?" Caroline snapped as they clung to the concrete rim. "You weren't even *trying* to swim."

"I don't know how," said Aria simply.

"Why would you offer to go up on the diving board if you don't know how to swim?"

"I didn't *know* I didn't know how to swim. I've never tried before. And I didn't expect to fall in."

"You could have drowned!"

"Oh," said Aria, thinking. "No, I don't think so."

Caroline let out an exasperated sound, and splashed water at her. And then despite herself, she laughed. Aria started laughing, too.

They were cut off sharply by a stern voice.

"What on *earth* are you girls doing?"

The laugh died in Caroline's throat as she looked up to see Mr. Cahill looming over them. She opened her mouth to explain, and so did Aria, but Mr. Cahill didn't give them a chance.

"Get out of the water," he snapped. "*Now.*"

Caroline and Aria sat in the headmistress's office, their hair still damp from the pool. Ms. Opeline had found them some dry clothes but the girls both looked pretty ragged. *Hardly the image of excellence and grace on the cover of the Westgate pamphlets*, thought Caroline.

Caroline sat perfectly still and stared straight ahead at the nametag on the headmistress's desk. When Aria noticed the sign, her eyes widened.

"Ms. Pierce?" she said aloud. "As in *Lily* Pierce?"

Caroline nodded. "The headmistress is her mom."

"Why didn't you tell me?" asked Aria.

"I didn't think it mattered."

Aria opened her mouth to say something more, but then the door opened, and Mr. Cahill walked in, followed by the headmistress.

Caroline had always been terrified of Ms. Pierce. She was dressed in a white blouse and black pants, and like Lily, she had perfect black hair and perfect teeth. But unlike Lily, Ms. Pierce never smiled. She took a seat, and rapped her manicured nails on the table as she considered them.

"I found the girls in the pool," said Mr. Cahill. "I don't know what possessed them to go in, but it wasn't even gym period, which means they were breaking half a dozen school rules, from swimming without supervision to skipping class to —"

"All right, Mr. Cahill," cut in Ms. Pierce. "I'll handle it from here. You can go back to the office."

The bespectacled man nodded and ducked out, mumbling ". . . kids these days . . ." as he went.

"So," said Ms. Pierce, "you two decided to go for a swim? During class?"

"I fell in," explained Aria. "Caroline dove in to save me."

"Is that true?" asked Ms. Pierce with a raised black brow. Caroline nodded. "But what were you doing out by the pool in the first place?" she pressed.

"Trying to get our uniforms back," said Aria. "Someone hung them from the diving board."

Ms. Pierce frowned and sat forward. "Do you know who?"

Aria started to speak, but Caroline cut her off. "No," she said. "It was just a stupid prank."

"Caroline Mason," said Ms. Pierce sternly. "If you know who did this, you need to *tell* me. Lying is a serious offense at Westgate." When Caroline said nothing, Ms. Pierce looked back at Aria. "Do *you* know who did it?"

Aria squirmed in her seat. She looked to Caroline, clearly confused, but finally shook her head.

"I can't hear you," pressed Ms. Pierce.

"No," said Aria, still looking at Caroline. "I don't know for sure who did it."

Someone knocked on the door, and a teacher stuck her head in. Ms. Pierce got up. "I'll be right back. Stay here."

The moment she was gone, Aria spun on Caroline.

"Why are you covering for her?" she hissed. "You *know* who put the clothes up there, Caroline."

"So?"

"So why won't you tell Ms. Pierce?" pressed Aria. "Lily's her daughter, so *tell her*. Tell her Lily is tormenting you. Tell her about the uniforms, and the locker, and . . ." Aria waved her hands emphatically. "Everything else," she said. "This is your chance."

Caroline looked down at her lap. It wasn't like she hadn't thought about it. It wasn't like she didn't want to. But she couldn't. If she did, it would all be over. There would be no going back. "No."

Aria looked at her, wide-eyed. "Why not?"

"If I tell on Lily, she'll never forgive me. She'll never . . ."

"Never what?"

Take me back, Caroline wanted to say.

"Caroline," said Aria. "Talk to me. I'm here to help, remember?"

Caroline looked up as it dawned on her. If Aria really was a guardian angel, then she *was* there to help. Aria could make things right. She straightened in her chair, and swallowed. "If you really are my guardian angel —"

"I am."

"— and you really do want to help me —"

"I do."

"Then help me get my old friends back."

chapter 16

ARIA

Aria stared at Caroline, dumbfounded.

After everything Lily had put her through, Caroline still wanted to be her friend?

Aria was at a loss. She *was* there to help, and Caroline had told her how she wanted her to help, but if this was how she was *supposed* to help, why did it feel so wrong?

"Well?" pressed Caroline.

Aria started to speak, but was saved by Ms. Pierce striding back in.

"Where were we?" she asked, taking her seat. "Ah, that's right. I'm giving you both Saturday school."

Aria's spirits rose at the prospect of something new but Caroline seemed upset.

"But it was an accident!" she cried.

"I'm sure it was, Miss Mason, but since you won't tell me who *is* responsible . . ." The headmistress paused again, waiting to see if Caroline had changed her mind, but she obviously hadn't. ". . . I have no choice. Rules were broken. There must be consequences. And if either of you decides to come back and tell me who *did* put those uniforms on the diving board, they'll be joining you on Saturday. In the meantime, I'll be notifying your parents."

Parents, thought Aria, biting her lip. She wasn't sure how *that* would go. She could magic up a clean school polo, or some pillows for the tree house. She didn't think she could magic up a mother and father.

"Miss Blue, there's no number listed on your information sheet," said Ms. Pierce, producing a crisp piece of paper. "In fact, there's nothing listed but a name. We must have had a technical malfunction. If you could fill out the rest . . ." She handed the paper to Aria, who stared down at the blank lines marked with things like *parents* and *address* and *home phone*. Her chest tightened a little, that strange dull sadness that floated up whenever she was reminded that she had nothing more than a name on a bracelet. And then she brushed it away, and filled in the blanks.

Her parents became *John* and *Kendall Blue* (she liked the names).

Her address — which in her head was *the blue-green tree house* — became *23 Tree House Lane*.

As for the phone number, Aria picked ten numbers — there were ten spots —at random, and then did her best to imagine a phone in her tree house to go with them.

The whole time she was writing, Caroline stared at the floor and listened to Ms. Pierce lecture her on the importance of honesty. "I have to say, I'm disappointed in you, Caroline. Integrity is an important part of Westgate's code. I depend on girls like you and Lily to be models of behavior."

A noise — somewhere between a sigh and a scoff — escaped through Aria's nose. Caroline shot her a look. Ms. Pierce didn't seem to notice.

"A Westgate girl," she continued, "does not lie, even to protect her friends."

"But why would Caroline's *friends* do something like this?" asked Aria pointedly. "Hanging our clothes up there was *mean*."

Ms. Pierce folded her hands, considering. "That's true. But why else would you protect them?"

"I'm not protecting anyone!" said Caroline. "I don't know who did it."

Ms. Pierce sighed, disappointed. "Very well. You two had best be getting to class, while there's still class left."

Caroline and Aria got to their feet and shuffled out. At the door, Aria paused and looked back. Ms. Pierce didn't seem like a very happy person. Aria thought maybe a bit of color would cheer her up. It certainly couldn't hurt, so she turned the little black bows on Ms. Pierce's black heels a sunny yellow.

"Is there something you want to say?" asked the headmistress, looking up. Aria only smiled, and shook her head, and followed Caroline out.

As soon as they were in the hallway, Caroline slumped against the wall. Aria touched her shoulder.

"So, will you help me?" asked Caroline.

Aria sighed. And whether she willed the bell overhead to ring, or it was simply time for lunch, the sound saved her from answering.

"Let's get some food," she said, hurrying away before Caroline could do anything but nod and follow.

But Caroline wouldn't let it go.

The first thing out of her mouth after they got their trays was, "Well? Are you going to help me?"

To which Aria said, "I'm starving." Even though she wasn't.

When they were standing in line, Caroline asked the question again. To which Aria said, "Should I get applesauce, or an orange?"

But once they sat down, there was no escape.

"Aria, are you going to help me get my friends back or not?"

Aria looked up, holding Caroline's gaze through the ring of blue smoke.

"No," she said.

Caroline frowned. "What do you mean, no?"

Aria hadn't used the word very often. She didn't even realize she was going to use it until it tumbled out. "No," she said again, "I can't do that. Or, I guess, I won't."

"I don't understand."

Aria thought about how to explain, that even though Caroline wanted to get her old friends back, it wasn't what she *needed*. There was a difference.

Yes, Aria could technically help Caroline get her friends back, but she knew in her bones and her shadow and the beginnings of her wings that it wouldn't help. It wouldn't make the blue smoke go away and it wouldn't make Caroline any happier. Going back wouldn't fix things. She had to go *forward*.

Aria was about to say this to Caroline, but Caroline didn't give her a chance.

"I thought you were supposed to be on my side," she said.

"I *am* on your side," insisted Aria.

"No, you're not." Caroline looked like she was about to cry. "You act like you're my friend, you say you're here to help me but you won't give me the only thing I want." She pushed up from the table. "What kind of a guardian angel are you?"

Aria felt like she'd been struck. "Caroline, listen . . ." she started, but the other girl was already storming away. Aria sighed. This could have been such a good day.

Now, sitting at the table by herself, the eyes of the other girls in the cafeteria turning toward her, Aria discovered how it felt to be abandoned. She could see her reflection in the waxy apple on her tray, distorted, but there. She poked her fingernail into the apple, drawing two small crescents just above the shoulders. Like wings.

What kind of guardian angel are you?

The single feather on her charm bracelet jingled faintly as she set the apple down, and stood up.

She was carrying the lunch trays to the return station when she heard Erica say, "Aw, did you two have a fight?"

Aria looked up to see Erica, Whitney, and Lily standing there.

"I told you not to waste your time on her," said Lily. "She's hopeless."

"She's a loser," added Whitney, a little halfheartedly.

Aria had had *enough*. "Why?" she asked Whitney. "Because she stood up for you?"

Whitney frowned. "What are you talking about?"

Aria felt her face get hot. "You were supposed to be Lily's victim this year. But Caroline stood up for you. That's why she is where she is, and you are where you are. Think about that the next time you decide to call her names."

Whitney looked at Lily and Erica, uncertainly. "Is . . . is that true?"

Erica rolled her eyes. "Whatever, it doesn't matter, Whit. Don't get worked up."

"You're one of us now," said Lily. "Isn't that what you want?"

Aria looked at Whitney. Whitney looked at the ground. Lily put her hand on Whitney's shoulder, and leaned in. "Do you want to go back to being a nobody?" she whispered in the girl's ear.

Whitney took a deep breath. Then she put on her best smile, looked at Aria, and said, "Caroline Mason is a nobody. I'm not."

Aria's heart sank. She remembered what Caroline had said that night on the trampoline. *Everyone just wants to belong.*

"You should have taken my advice," chided Lily.

Why? Aria wanted to ask. *Why are you doing this?*

"She didn't turn you in, you know," Aria told Lily. "After what you did with our uniforms. She wouldn't."

Lily shrugged, even though her blue smoke swirled violently around her shoulders.

"I feel sorry for her," said Aria.

"Because she's an outcast?" jabbed Erica.

"No." Aria shook her head. "Because even after all you've done to her, she'd come running back to you. I feel sorry for her," she said, "because she can't see that none of you are worth it."

And with that, Aria dumped the trays, and went to find Caroline.

chapter 17

CAROLINE

Caroline sat in the stairwell, her knees drawn up. She didn't know how long she'd been sitting there — it was still lunch — but she was about to drag herself to her feet when she felt her cell phone buzz in her backpack. She frowned and dug it out. Caroline's cell phone hadn't buzzed with a text — at least one that wasn't from her mom or sister — in weeks.

The message was from Lily.

I miss you, it said. *Come over after school. Pool party. Like old times.*

Her chest started to ache. Did Lily really want her back? Had she gotten bored of tormenting Caroline? Or was this just another prank?

I'm not falling for it, she texted back.

But a second later, the phone buzzed again. *Come on, Car.* Caroline could picture Lily draping her arm around her shoulders, resting her black curls against Caroline's straight blond hair. *Please come. We can talk.*

Caroline read the texts once, then twice, then a dozen more times before the stairwell door swung open. Without looking up, she knew it was Aria. Maybe it was the way the overhead light brightened slightly, or the faint jingle of the girl's charm bracelet.

"Look," said Aria, sitting down beside her. "I'm trying to understand where you're coming from."

Caroline shook her head. Aria *couldn't* understand. Had she ever been a person before she was an angel? Had she ever had best friends? The kind you love even when you don't like them? The kind you miss even when they make you miserable? "I only want things to go back to the way they were."

"Do you think they can?" asked Aria.

Caroline's stomach tightened.

"Do you think they *should*?" pressed Aria. "Look at science. Things move forward. Not back."

"I wish you would just help me," said Caroline.

"I'm *trying*," said Aria. "But it seems to me like Lily Pierce is a bully. The girls who hang out with her are bullies."

"I'd rather be a bully than a nobody," mumbled Caroline.

"You act like those are the only two options," said Aria, sounding exasperated. "Like there's nothing in between. But there are so many things between, Caroline. There's nice. And funny. Kind. Smart. Strange. Cool . . . And there are girls at this school who are those things. They may not be the most *popular*, but they're not nobodies."

Caroline swallowed hard. "It doesn't matter. Even if I wanted to make new friends, all the other girls ignore me."

Aria shook her head. "No," she said. "A few of them ignore you. *You're* ignoring everyone else. You act like Lily is the only person at Westgate worth being friends *with*. But this school is full of other people. I can help you find them."

Caroline's eyes burned. She didn't want to start over. She just wanted to go back. Back to the moment when she tried to stop Lily from pranking Whitney. She would do everything differently.

Suddenly, Aria's face brightened. "Ah!" she said, "Why didn't I think of this before?"

"Think of what?"

"We'll let my shadow decide!"

Caroline had no idea what Aria was talking about. "How is your shadow supposed to help?"

"Because it's not *just* a shadow," explained Aria. "It's also a door."

"A door . . ." echoed Caroline, confused.

Aria nodded. "One that takes me wherever I'm supposed to be. Which means it will take *you* wherever you're supposed to be. So if we go through, and it takes us to Lily, I'll help you get your old friends back." Caroline's spirits lifted. "But," added Aria, "you have to promise me that if it takes us somewhere else, you'll let me help you *my* way."

Caroline hesitated. She thought of Lily's texts and stared down at the shadow beneath Aria's feet. "Does it ever make the wrong choice?" she asked.

Aria shook her head. "No."

Caroline took a deep breath. "Okay," she said. "Deal."

Aria broke into a grin, and hopped up. "Let's go."

"We can't go *now*," said Caroline. "Lunch is almost over."

"We won't be gone long," Aria assured her. And then she looked down and tapped her foot a few times. Her shadow turned on like a light. The same light that had surrounded Aria when Caroline almost fell down the stairs.

Caroline gasped. If she didn't believe before, she was starting to now. . . .

Aria held out her hand. "Come on."

Caroline stood up and surveyed the pool of light on the ground. She took Aria's hand, squeezed her eyes shut, and stepped through.

A second later, Caroline opened her eyes. All she saw were trees, and fences, and sky. She wasn't at school. The ground wobbled under her feet, and when she looked down, she saw that they were standing on the trampoline in her backyard.

Caroline's heart sank. She realized how badly she'd wanted the shadow door to take them to Lily. But why had it taken them *here*?

"I don't understand," she said, turning on Aria. "What does this mean?"

Aria bounced a little on her toes, considering the trampoline. "I'm not sure."

Caroline sighed. "This doesn't tell me anything."

"Well," said Aria, "It didn't take you to Lily . . ." Caroline's throat tightened. She felt Aria's hand on her shoulder. "It's for the best."

Caroline nodded numbly. "We'd better get back to school."

Aria snapped her fingers, and the light blossomed at their feet. An instant later they were back in the stairwell, as if nothing had happened. The light went out, and Aria's shadow was nothing more than an ordinary stretch of darkness on the floor.

"Are you all right?" asked Aria.

"A deal's a deal," said Caroline, hollowly.

The bell rang overhead, and Aria turned toward the door. When Caroline didn't follow, she looked back. "Are you coming? It's time for science."

"You go ahead," said Caroline. "I'll catch up in a second."

She waited for Aria to leave, and then she dug her cell phone from her bag and read Lily's texts one last time.

Come on, Car.

Maybe Aria had lied about the shadow taking her where she *needed* to go. Maybe it only went where Aria *wanted*. After all, she didn't want Lily and Caroline to be friends again. She didn't understand.

Please come.

Caroline chewed her lip, and then typed one word — *OK* — and hit send.

Caroline's bikini was blue and green and white.

Lily had picked it out for her over the summer. She and Lily and Erica had spent a whole day at the mall, trying on bikinis and one-pieces.

"Car!" Lily had cried when Caroline tried on this bikini. "You're like summer on a stick! It has to be that one! Look," she said, holding up her own choice, blue and white, "we match!"

Erica had picked out an orange one-piece, but when she saw theirs, she shoved it back onto the rack and chose a green one instead. Lily had smiled and patted Erica's hair. "Perfect. Now we *all* match."

Caroline checked herself in the mirror now. For an instant, she wondered if she *shouldn't* head over to Lily's. But then she pulled on a pair of shorts, slung a towel over her shoulder, and went downstairs. Her mom, dad, and Megan were in the kitchen.

"Where do you think you're going?" asked her mom, who was *not* happy about the Saturday school news. "Haven't you had enough swimming for one day?"

"Oh, what did Car do now?" asked Megan.

"She got herself a weekend detention after skipping class to go for a swim."

"It wasn't like that," said Caroline.

"Nicely done, little sis!" said Megan in a rare display of affection.

"Megan, don't encourage her," said her dad. But then he

smiled. "Not that Westgate doesn't need to loosen up a little."

"Was it Aria's idea?" asked her mom.

"No," Caroline tried to explain for the zillionth time, "it wasn't *anybody's* idea. She fell in; I had to go get her because she can't swim."

Oh yeah, and she's also apparently my guardian angel.

Caroline thought it best not to mention that part.

"That's not nearly as cool," said Megan, pulling out her phone.

"Yeah, well, it's the only reason your sister isn't *grounded for life*," said Caroline's mom.

"So can I go or not?" asked Caroline.

"Where are you going?" asked her dad.

"Lily's."

Her mom's face broke into a smile. "I'm so glad you two are making up," she said. "Is Aria going with you?"

Caroline shook her head. Of course she hadn't told Aria what she was doing.

"Have fun," said her dad.

"Be home by eight," added her mom.

Caroline walked across the lawn, and up Lily's front steps. She could hear music and laughter and splashing in the backyard, sounds of summer, of good days. She closed her eyes, took a deep breath, and rang the bell.

No one answered.

She rang the bell again.

Again, nothing.

Caroline's heart started to race, but she told herself it was fine. They probably couldn't hear her, with the music turned up. She went around to the back fence door, the one that led straight to the backyard, and pulled on it.

It was locked.

Caroline hesitated. She could still hear the music, and the slosh of water, but the chatter had stopped.

She was about to knock.

And then she heard the giggle.

It wasn't loud, but soft and stifled, as if someone had put their hand over their mouth. It was coming from right on the other side of the door. Lily and Erica and Whitney were there. And they were hiding from her.

Caroline was standing in Lily's yard in a blue and green and white bikini.

And she felt like an idiot.

Because of course things weren't going back to the way they were before. They were never going back. Lily wasn't her best friend anymore.

She didn't miss her.

She just wanted another chance to humiliate her.

And Caroline had fallen for it, because she hadn't wanted to believe it was really over.

It took all of her strength not to start crying right there. She turned and padded back across the lawn toward her house, tears streaming silently down her face. But halfway there, she slowed, and stopped.

She couldn't go home. Not yet. Her family had just watched her leave, and if she came back now, she'd have to tell them *why*.

But she couldn't just stand there either, so she crossed the street to a giant tree in her neighbor's front yard. And when she was on the far side of the tree, hidden from view, she sank down among the roots and sobbed.

A few moments later, she felt arms fold around her, and with them a strange, familiar comfort.

Aria said nothing, not "I told you so" or "you should have known" or "how could you be so stupid?" Instead she just sat there with her arms wrapped around Caroline's shoulders, and let her cry.

chapter 18

ARIA

Aria had seen it all.

She'd had a bad feeling something was going to happen — Caroline had been quiet all afternoon, her smoke thickening around her. So after school, Aria had sat at the windowsill of the tree house, watching, willing Caroline not to do it, and knowing that she couldn't stop her. That was the problem with being a guardian angel. You were there to help someone, but they had to *want* that help. They had to be ready for it. And apparently Caroline Mason wasn't quite ready for it yet.

It was still hard to watch.

Now, Caroline buried her face in Aria's shoulder. "I'm so stupid," she whispered. Her voice hitched from crying.

"No, you're not," said Aria, hugging her tighter.

"All I wanted was to get my life back." *Hitch.* "All I had was that. I don't know how" — *hitch* — "to move on."

"It's going to be okay," Aria whispered into Caroline's hair. Not "it's okay," because it wasn't yet. But it would be.

"How do you know?" asked Caroline, pulling back.

"Because I'm here to make sure of it," said Aria honestly. "Caroline, I wouldn't be here if I *couldn't* help you. And I'm not going anywhere until I have, okay?"

Caroline pulled the towel around her, and used a corner to wipe her eyes. "Okay," she said quietly. She leaned back against the tree and sniffled, and the two sat there for a few minutes like that, wrapped in Caroline's smoke and Aria's comfort.

"Where did you come from?" asked Caroline, breaking the quiet.

Aria's brows went up. She wasn't sure how to answer that. "You mean like, in the beginning?"

Caroline let out a small, tired laugh. "No, I mean, just now."

"Oh." Aria looked up. "There."

"The sky?" asked Caroline.

Aria smiled. "No, silly. The tree house."

Caroline seemed to notice it for the first time. "Oh."

"Come on," said Aria, tugging the girl to her feet. "I'll show you."

Aria led Caroline past a small sign that read *23 Tree House Lane* — she was quite pleased with that addition — and to the rope ladder. Caroline hesitated, and Aria remembered her fear of heights.

"How can you love the sky and the stars and be afraid of heights?" Aria asked. "Isn't space the highest thing there is?"

"It's different," said Caroline, looking up through the tree limbs. "Space is so high up I don't really think of it as high. Just far away." She wrapped her fingers around the rope ladder. "In space, there's no gravity. That's what I'm afraid of. Falling."

"I won't let you fall," said Aria.

Caroline looked at her, for the first time without doubt, and said, "I know."

And then slowly she started to climb. Aria waited until she was at the top, and then followed her up. Inside the tree house, Caroline got to her feet (a little shakily), then broke into a smile.

"You okay?" Aria asked.

"Still in one piece," Caroline said. And then her eyes widened. "Whoa," she said, looking around. "This is where you live?"

Aria nodded. "For now."

"So this guardian angel thing," said Caroline, "it doesn't come with a house, or a family, or a fake identity, like if you were a spy?"

"No," said Aria, picking at the hem of her skirt. "Just me."

"That's got to be hard."

Aria shrugged.

Caroline noticed the picture of herself and Lily tacked to the wall. She traced her fingers along the blue lines that wrapped around them.

"What's that?" she asked.

"Smoke," said Aria. "You look at you and just see you," she explained. "When *I* look at you, I see blue smoke around you. It's how I found you. How I knew you were the one I was supposed to help."

Caroline's hand fell away as she turned back to Aria. "So what are we going to do about Lily?"

"Nothing," said Aria.

Caroline frowned. "What do you mean? There has to be a way to get revenge."

Aria understood the urge. She'd certainly been tempted to pull a few magical pranks, but bullying bullies didn't seem like the right answer.

"You told me I needed to stand up for myself," Caroline pointed out.

"There's a difference between standing up for yourself and getting even. Besides, this isn't about fighting back. It's about moving on. Are you really ready to move on?" pressed Aria. "To make new friends? Because I can help you," she said. "If you're willing to let me."

Caroline swallowed. And then she nodded. "Okay," she said. "I'm ready."

And as she said it, Caroline's smoke finally started to thin.

Aria and Caroline sat in the tree house until dark, stretched out on the floor, watching the sunset through the branches, and talking.

And the longer they talked, the more Aria became convinced that Caroline — not the version of her who had followed Lily's orders, or the version who'd been lost in space the last few weeks, but Caroline as she was under all of that — was great. She was funny and she was smart, and full of random facts like how far they were from the moon, and why it was so bright, and what the constellations were called. Aria loved learning all this. It made the world seem even more magical.

"Hey, Aria?" said Caroline when it was dark and they could see the stars.

"Yeah, Caroline?"

"I think I know why your shadow took me to the trampoline today."

"Why's that?"

"Well, I go out there to look at stars. It's always been the place I feel most like *me*," she said. "Lily and I were on the trampoline when she told me that it was more important to be popular than be myself. And I believed her."

"And now?" asked Aria in the dark.

"Now I want people to like me for *me*. Do you think that's possible?"

Aria smiled. "Absolutely."

When it was almost 8:00 p.m., Aria walked Caroline home.

"See you in the morning?" asked Aria when they reached her door.

"Yeah," said Caroline. "It'll be a fresh start. Caroline 2.0."

Aria cocked her head. "I don't know what that means."

Caroline smiled. "It's like, when you have a computer, and you update the software. Same person, new version."

Aria thought about it a long moment. "Yes!" she announced. "Like that."

She wondered, as she walked away, if she was Aria 2.0, too.

Aria found her feet carrying her across the lawn, and through the white picket fence to the Pierces's house. She took a deep breath, and made herself invisible before approaching the kitchen window.

Erica and Whitney and Lily were standing around the counter, their hair wet from the pool. But Lily didn't seem happy. Her hand went to her collar, as if reaching for a necklace. Weird. Aria had seen Caroline do the exact same thing.

"Come on," said Erica, "you have to admit it was funny."

"That's not the point," snapped Lily. "You shouldn't have used my phone."

"Well, I couldn't exactly use *my* phone. Caroline would never have come. She's not *that* stupid."

"I still can't believe she fell for it," chimed in Whitney. There was a new meanness in her voice. As if she was trying to prove that she fit in.

"Yeah, well, she did," said Lily, sounding put out.

"You're no fun today," said Erica, resting her head on Lily's shoulder. Lily shrugged her off.

"Hey," said Erica, scrambling. "What are we wearing to the dance next week?"

"I don't care," said Lily. "I have a headache. And homework. I'll see you tomorrow."

The two girls stared at her, clearly shocked by her cold tone.

"Are you mad?" asked Whitney with a pout.

Lily mustered up a smile that Aria could tell was fake. "No," she said. "Of course not."

But as soon as Erica and Whitney were gone, Lily slumped down at the kitchen table, her smoke swirling darkly around her shoulders. She looked miserable. And lonely.

Aria didn't get it.

Why was Lily tormenting Caroline? And if she didn't want to do it anymore, why didn't she simply tell the other girls to stop? What was she afraid of?

Aria remembered Caroline's words.

I'd rather be a bully than a nobody.

Was Lily scared of losing her place at the top?

Aria was about to leave when Lily dug her hand in her pocket and pulled out a necklace. She held it up to the light, and Aria saw a silver pendant on the end of a chain. It looked like half of a circle. Lily stared at it for several long moments, then put it back in her pocket.

chapter 19

CAROLINE

Caroline was halfway to her bedroom when she heard her sister's voice.

"Hey, Car, get in here."

Considering Megan spent most of her life keeping Caroline *out* of her room, the order made her nervous. She hovered on the threshold, racking her brain. Had she borrowed anything? Broken anything?

"Sit," said Megan, pointing to her bed. "I'll braid your hair."

Growing up, Megan played with Caroline's hair all the time. But it had been years since she'd offered to do it. Still, as Caroline climbed onto her sister's bed and Megan drew the brush through her hair, Caroline began to feel sleepy and safe.

"Talk to me," said Megan.

"Why?" asked Caroline.

"Because I'm your big sister. Because you used to ramble in my ear about every little thing in your life. Because I know something's up with you and Lily, and I can tell you didn't go swimming." Caroline looked down at her lap. "What's going on with you?" asked Megan. There was no accusation, no jab in her tone. It was the closest thing she had come to sounding concerned.

"We're not friends anymore," said Caroline. It hurt her throat to say it. "We haven't been for a while."

Megan set aside the brush, and moved to face her sister. "I know it hurts. I know it feels awful and huge and like it will never really get better. But it will."

"How do you know?" asked Caroline quietly.

"Because it's the way life works. I wish I could tell you that every friendship lasts forever, but it doesn't. People change. Sometimes for the better, sometimes for the worse." Megan brought her hand to rest on Caroline's head. "The trick is remembering who *you* are. But I'm sorry things have been hard, Car."

Caroline nodded, and wrapped her arms around her sister. "Thanks, Megan."

"No problem," she said. "Now get out of my room."

• • •

"I'm not ready," said Caroline the next morning.

She'd gone to bed feeling ready and woken up feeling sick. It was one thing to *say* you were ready in the safety of a tree house at night, and another to *be* ready surrounded by girls you were pretty sure wanted nothing to do with you.

"You are," insisted Aria. They were in gym class, passing a soccer ball back and forth on the field.

"I can't do this."

"Yes," said Aria. "You can. It's easy. We're passing a soccer ball, they're passing a soccer ball, everyone's passing soccer balls. You have something in common already! Let's go see if we can join another group."

Caroline groaned. Aria made it sound so easy. Like it was the first day of school. Like the whole grade didn't hate her, or at least fear Lily's wrath enough to pretend they did. Caroline never used to be shy, but now her nerves rattled in her chest.

"When people think about you," said Aria, "they think about you and Lily. You have to get them to see who *you* are outside of her."

"But how? No one will even talk to me."

"Have you talked to *them*?" asked Aria.

Caroline opened and closed her mouth, but said nothing.

130

Aria sighed and kicked the ball back to her. "What are you afraid of, Caroline? That they'll say no?"

"That's exactly what I'm afraid of." Caroline kicked the ball back hard. "And then I'll look even more pathetic."

"Did it ever occur to you," said Aria, stopping the ball, "that not everyone here cares about your fight with Lily? That even though it feels really big to you, maybe it's not the center of *their* universe?" Aria picked the ball up. "Maybe they're not all talking about you behind your back. Maybe some of them are even waiting for *you* to make an effort."

Caroline looked over at the other groups of girls laughing and chatting and passing the ball. She wanted to believe Aria, but . . .

"You don't believe me, do you?" asked Aria. She crinkled her brow, thinking. And then she broke into a smile, and looked around. "Come on," she said, dropping the ball back to the grass. "I have an idea."

Caroline followed Aria off the field, and over the track, and around the corner of the building. "I don't know if this will work," Aria said.

"If what will work?"

"Give me your hand."

"Why?" asked Caroline, suspicious.

"Trust me," said Aria, and Caroline did. She took Aria's hand. "Now, don't freak out."

"What would I freak out abou —" But the words fell away as Caroline saw their hands, followed by the rest of them, *disappear*.

"Hey, it worked," came Aria's voice, even though Caroline couldn't see Aria. Or herself.

"What did you do?" whispered Caroline, her pulse racing. Were they *invisible*?

"Come on," said Aria, and Caroline could feel herself being pulled back toward the soccer field. "I want you to hear what people are saying."

It was kind of cool to be invisible — to be *actually, magically* invisible, and not just *feel* invisible and ignored. But Caroline also had a bad feeling about this. As they wove through the groups of girls, she braced herself for gossip, expecting to hear her name on everyone's tongues.

But to Caroline's surprise, no one was talking about her. Most of the girls were talking about their weekend plans, or the upcoming dance with Eastgate, or how eager they were for gym to be over.

And then, finally, she heard her name mentioned. Not by Lily or her group (Lily seemed off today, quieter than usual) but by a girl named Ginny. She had sun-streaked hair and a band of freckles across her nose, and Caroline didn't know much about her except that she was on a local swim team.

"I'm just saying," Ginny was rambling to her friend, a dark-haired girl named Elle, "that I think Caroline Mason seems pretty cool."

"Drama," said Elle. Caroline cringed. "Way too much drama. And it's not worth wading into it, not with Lily Pierce in the mix."

Ginny scoffed. "Like I care what Lily thinks."

"Don't let *her* hear you say that. . . ."

Caroline was so shocked — by the fact that someone thought she was cool, and the fact that they weren't afraid of Lily — that she didn't even notice that the bell had rung until Aria was dragging her toward the lockers.

Caroline asked Aria if they could stay invisible for the rest of the day, but Aria said no. Aria also said Caroline had to try sitting at a new table at lunch. No more Table 12.

Now Caroline stood in the cafeteria, her heart hammering in her chest. "Couldn't you just summon up some friends for me?" she asked Aria, only half joking.

"No," said Aria, handing her a tray.

Some guardian angel, thought Caroline, staring out at the sea of tables that waited past the checkout. "This isn't going to work," she said again.

"Of course it is," said Aria, setting a vanilla pudding cup on her tray. "Eleven tables. Infinite opportunities for friendship."

"Infinite opportunities for embarrassment," mumbled Caroline. "You act like I can just *magically* make new friends."

"It's not magic," insisted Aria. "The problem is you've never looked beyond your group. Lucky for you, there are tons of girls at this school worth being friends with." Aria looked around the lunchroom. "You see the two girls at Table Eight?" she said. "Jasmine and Nora? They run a music blog. Renée and Amanda at Table Two want to be in the World Cup someday, whatever that is. The girls at Table Six are all in drama or dance, and half the girls at Table Four are in the science club, and the girls at Table Ten want to start a band, but they can never seem to settle on a name."

Caroline looked at her, wide-eyed. "How do you *know* all of that?"

"Because I *listened*," said Aria. "I paid attention."

"You were also probably invisible."

"The point is," said Aria, "maybe it's time for you to start listening. Get to know them," she pressed. "Let them get to know you."

Caroline took a deep breath and stepped forward without looking, accidentally bumping into a girl in front of her. "Sorry," she said quickly.

The girl glanced back. "No worries," she said. It wasn't just any girl. It was Ginny, from the soccer field.

Normally, the conversation would be over, but Caroline thought about what Aria had said, about listening, and paying attention, and how *she* had been the one doing most of the ignoring.

"Hey," continued Caroline. "You're a swimmer, aren't you?"

Ginny raised a brow. She shot a glance across the cafeteria toward Table 7 — toward Lily — but then nodded and said, "Yeah. Backstroke." Ginny paused and said, "You like to swim, too, don't you?"

Caroline brightened. "How did you know?"

Ginny gave her a crooked smile. "I heard you got a Saturday school for cutting class to take a swim. Is that true?"

Caroline groaned. "Yeah. Kind of. I mean, not really."

The line moved forward and so did they. "I did go in the pool, but I didn't really have a choice."

"I can't swim," said Aria behind her. "I fell in, and Caroline jumped in and pulled me out."

Ginny's eyes widened. "Whoa, is that true?"

They hit the checkout, paid, and made their way toward the tables.

"It's no big deal," said Caroline.

"She totally saved my life," said Aria. "You should have seen it!"

Ginny smiled. "That's pretty cool," she said as they reached her table. "Hey, Elle," she said to the dark-haired girl already sitting down. "Did you know Caroline here saved Aria's life?"

"No way," said Elle, looking up.

"Yes way," said Aria. "I almost drowned. Lucky for me Caroline's a good swimmer."

Caroline blushed. A few other girls turned toward her, and she realized they were hovering at the edge of Table 2.

"Well?" said Ginny. "You want to sit down?"

Caroline spent the rest of lunch telling the girls at Table 2 about the swimming pool incident. It didn't help that Aria kept making the story bigger, the diving board higher, the fall more dangerous, the fear of drowning ever-present (even though Caroline was pretty sure the guardian angel could have stayed underwater for days and been perfectly fine).

"Yeah," said Elle, "but what were you guys doing by the pool in the first place?"

Caroline glanced across the cafeteria at Table 7, and was surprised to find Lily staring at her.

"*Someone,*" said Aria, "stole our uniforms, and hung them on top of the diving board."

Ginny rolled her eyes. "This school."

The bell rang, and for the first time in weeks, Caroline didn't want lunch to end. It had been so nice to have a table to sit at. To have people to talk to. And then, as they all got up to clear their trays, Caroline overheard Elle whisper in Ginny's ear. "Did you see the way Lily was looking at us?"

Caroline's chest twisted, but Ginny only shrugged.

"Let her look," said Ginny. "If she hangs *my* clothes from the diving board, I'll go and get them down."

"Try not to fall in," said Aria earnestly.

The girls broke into laughter, and Caroline let out a sigh of relief. Aria was right. Apparently not everyone at Westgate worshipped at the altar of Lily Pierce.

"Hey," said Ginny, turning to Caroline, "want to sit with us tomorrow?"

Aria beamed, and Caroline felt like she was glowing from the inside out. "I'd love to."

Her heart raced when she said it. Not with fear, but excitement. It felt like the first day of school. Like the first day of *life*.

It felt, she realized, like a fresh start.

chāpter 20

ARIA

That night, Aria sat in her tree house, trying to decide what to do. She fiddled with her charm bracelet as her mind drifted, like smoke, through the problem. Caroline was on her way, but Lily —

A car door slammed across the street. Aria watched as Lily Pierce got out and went inside her house, tendrils of blue smoke trailing behind her like a cape.

While Caroline's smoke was thinning, Lily's was thicker than ever. It coiled around her, the way it had the night before, when she snapped at Erica and Whitney. The way it had at lunch that day, when Caroline smiled and laughed with Ginny and Elle.

Aria knew she was supposed to be helping Lily, too. But how? She'd tried to talk to her in the hallway at school that afternoon, but Lily made it clear that she wanted nothing to do with her. She walked right past Aria, as if she were invisible, even though she wasn't (Aria had checked to make sure).

Aria heard someone padding toward the tree. She got up, expecting Caroline, but as the rope ladder groaned under the person's weight, Aria could tell it wasn't her.

She had just enough time to make herself invisible before a small blond head popped up through the space in the floor. It was a boy. His eyes went wide. Aria may have made herself vanish, but she hadn't vanished anything else, not the pillows or the schoolbag or the phone or the pretty twinkling lights.

The boy looked around and took a deep breath. "*Mooooom!*" he called out at the top of his lungs, before disappearing back through the hole in the floor. "Mom!" Aria heard him shouting as he ran across the lawn. "Someone is living in my tree house! A *girl* is living in my tree house!"

As soon as he was gone, Aria snapped her fingers, and the pillows and the schoolbag and the phone and the pretty twinkling lights disappeared one by one, like candle flames. By the time the boy managed to drag his mother out of the house, across the lawn, and up the ladder, the tree house was as empty — only a beanbag and a shelf — as she'd found it. Aria perched on the windowsill and crossed her arms, invisible.

"Jamie," said his mom, exasperated, "what on earth has gotten into you?"

"There was someone's stuff here!" exclaimed the boy. "I swear —"

"You and your imagination."

"But I *swear* —"

"Enough. This is why you can't have candy before bed." And with that, she dragged him away.

Aria sighed and became visible again. One by one, her things flickered back into sight. The last twinkling light reappeared just as she heard Caroline call from the base of the ladder and start climbing up.

"You're getting better at that!" said Aria as Caroline hoisted herself up into the tree house.

"I am," said Caroline, only a little shaky. "As long as I don't look down . . ."

Aria smiled. And then she saw the plastic box under Caroline's arm. "What's that?"

Caroline held up the container. "Cookies," she said. "Mom made them. I hope you like chocolate chip."

Aria had yet to find a kind of cookie she *didn't* like. The two girls sat on the tree house floor and ate. But Aria could feel her attention tugging now and then toward Lily's house. She fiddled with her charm bracelet again.

"How come it only has one charm?" asked Caroline.

"I have to earn the rest," said Aria.

"What do you mean?"

"Do you see these three rings?" asked Aria, pointing to the small metal circles on her bracelet. "Every time I help someone, I get a feather on one of them."

"Ah, so you're, like, literally earning your wings."

Aria nodded. "I earned my first feather," she said, touching the small silver pendant, "for helping a girl named Gabby. And once I help you, I'll earn another feather. But see how this ring is different?" She held it up so Caroline could see the way the middle ring was actually two rings, intertwined. "That's because you're not the only one I'm supposed to be helping here."

"Who else . . ." started Caroline. And then her eyes went to the photo on the wall, the one with threads of blue smoke wrapping not just around Caroline, but around Lily, too. "No," Caroline said quietly. "No way."

"I don't pick who I'm here to help."

Caroline jumped to her feet, her face red. "But why would *Lily Pierce* need a guardian angel?"

"I don't know." Aria sighed. "And I don't know how to help her."

"You told me this was about me," said Caroline. "But it's about us, isn't it? Both of us. Maybe if you help one of us, the other will get better."

"That's what I thought," said Aria. "That's what I hoped. But your smoke is getting better, and Lily's smoke is getting worse. And she doesn't seem to *want* my help."

And then Aria froze, a cookie halfway to her mouth. She repeated the line in her head, only this time she changed the emphasis. *She doesn't seem to want* my *help.*

But what about Caroline's? Maybe Aria wasn't supposed to help Lily, not directly. Maybe she was supposed to help *Caroline* so *she* could help Lily.

"Lily's always been stubborn," Caroline was saying, shaking her head. "I still care about her, I guess. Even after all she's done. Even though we can't be friends. It's weird, isn't it? I like her, even though she obviously hates me."

"I don't think she hates you," said Aria. "I think she's lost."

"Part of me never wants to see her again," said Caroline, "but the rest of me wishes we could just *talk*. One on one. Without Erica and Whitney and everyone else watching."

A light went off inside Aria's head. She smiled and took another cookie. "Maybe you can."

chapter 21

CAROLINE

Caroline half expected it all to be a dream. Or worse, another prank. She thought she'd get to lunch on Friday, and sit down at Table 2, and Ginny and Elle and Renée and Amanda would look at her like she was crazy. But they didn't. When she brought her tray over, Ginny looked up and grinned at her.

Relief poured over Caroline and she sat down.

"There you are," said Ginny. "We were just talking about you."

Caroline's smile faltered. "You were?"

"Yeah," chimed in Elle. "We're having a sleepover on Friday. Do you want to come?"

Caroline brightened. "Really?" she asked, a little too excited.

"Relax," said Elle. "It's just a sleepover."

144

"Yeah," said Renée. "It'll be fun. Movies. Popcorn. Pillow forts."

Caroline's spirits lifted. "Can I bring Aria?" she asked, pointing back toward the lunch line, where the guardian angel was holding Jell-O cups up to the light.

The girls at Table 2 looked Aria's way, and for a moment, it was like they'd forgotten who she was. Like she'd slipped out of their minds (which was weird, because Aria was the brightest, boldest thing in Caroline's life). It wasn't the first time it had happened. Caroline had asked Aria about it, and Aria had only shrugged and said, "People notice me when they need to."

But after a second of staring, Ginny shrugged and said, "Sure."

"Give me your phone," said Elle. "I'll put in the address."

Caroline pulled her phone out and passed it to Elle as Aria finally came over and sat down.

"You want to come to a sleepover tonight?" Caroline asked Aria, eyes pleading. Nothing would go wrong if Aria was with her.

"Sure," said Aria with a smile, and then a second later, "What's a sleepover?"

The girls at the table looked at her like she was an alien. Which wasn't too far off. "You know," said Caroline, nudging

Aria with her elbow. "Where everyone gets together at some-one's house and plays games and *sleeps over*."

"Oh . . ." said Aria. "Oh, yeah, of course. Obviously."

"Great," said Ginny. "Oh, and bring a swimsuit," she added.

Caroline stiffened. "Why?"

"I have a pool and the weather is supposed to be warm," she said. She looked over at Aria. "You going to be okay? There's a shallow end. We can teach you how to swim."

Aria beamed. "That would be great," she said. "I know how to float, but only underwater."

The girls laughed, but Caroline felt a ripple of panic roll through her. She saw herself standing in front of Lily's house in her blue and green and white bikini. Heard herself knocking on the door, and the muffled giggle on the other side, and —

Then Aria squeezed her arm. Caroline blinked, and the memory dissolved.

"We'll be there," Aria was saying. "We can't wait."

"You've never been to a sleepover?" asked Caroline as they walked to class.

Aria shook her head. "There are a lot of things I haven't done."

"Like what?"

Aria shrugged. "How do I know if I haven't done them?"

"Well," said Caroline. "Have you been to the ocean?" Aria shook her head. "Eaten pizza? Been to a dance? Had a crush on a boy?"

Aria blushed. "No."

"We're going to have to work on that," said Caroline. They passed Ms. Opeline's office. She was standing in the doorway, and smiled at Caroline as they went past. Caroline smiled back, but kept walking.

"Are you excited about tonight?" asked Aria.

"I'm nervous," admitted Caroline. "It's just . . . what if . . ." *What if it's all a trap? What if they don't like me? What if . . .*

"You have to give people a chance," said Aria. "They're giving *you* a chance, aren't they?" It was true. Ginny and Elle didn't have to invite her along. "Besides," said Aria, "they might surprise you."

But that's what Caroline was afraid of. She felt like she was walking through a booby-trapped world, waiting for the mines to go off.

. . .

Friday after school, Aria sat cross-legged on Caroline's bed while Caroline packed an overnight bag, stressing over every single hair clip and sock.

"Sleepovers are supposed to be fun, right?" asked Aria, fiddling with her laces, which she'd turned bright blue.

"Yeah," murmured Caroline, dumping out her bag for the fifth time and starting over.

"So why do you look so miserable?"

Caroline sighed. "I'm not. I just . . . I want to get this right." After spending the whole week in a uniform, picking out regular clothes seemed impossible. What should she wear? What would *they* wear?

"Just be you," said Aria, hopping down off the bed. "Here, close your eyes."

Caroline sighed and did as Aria said.

"If no one was going to see you, what would you wear?"

Caroline started to say that it was a stupid question, since people *were* going to see her, but she stopped herself and tried to think of an answer. On weekends, around the house, she usually wore jeans and a T-shirt. Her favorite was this shirt with a galaxy on the front. It was soft from wear, but the colors were still bright. And she had these pink flats that

Lily had told her were out of style, so Caroline had stopped wearing them.

Caroline kept her eyes closed as she told Aria about the outfit. She felt a breeze around her, a flutter of fabric, and when she blinked and looked down, she was wearing the clothes, just as she'd described them, which was amazing because she'd lost that galaxy shirt three months ago.

"How . . ." started Caroline, but she realized it was a silly thing to ask a girl who could make things out of nothing. Instead she smiled and said, "Thanks, Aria. I feel . . ." She looked down at her shoes. "Like me."

Aria beamed, and the lights in the room brightened. Then Aria summoned up a new outfit for herself, too — pink jeans and a bright blue top.

Caroline checked her watch and groaned. "We're going to be late." Her parents were really happy that Caroline was going to a sleepover, but they weren't home yet to drive the girls over. And walking would take a while.

Aria's smile widened. "Don't worry," she said. "I know a shortcut."

She snapped her fingers, and her shadow turned on like a light.

•   •   •

Aria's shadow put them out in front of a pretty yellow house with a green door. Aria reattached her shadow while Caroline stared up at the house as if it might eat her.

Don't think of Lily's. Don't think of Lily's. Don't think of Lily's, she willed herself, even though she couldn't *not* think of Lily's place.

"After you," said Aria. Caroline took the lead, and Aria followed her up the front steps. When they reached the door, she took a deep breath, and willed herself to ring the bell.

At first, no one answered.

Oh no, thought Caroline. *No. No.* It was going to be like Lily's place all over again.

"This was a mistake," said Caroline, taking a step back. "Maybe we should —"

And then the door swung open, and Ginny stood there, breathless.

"Sorry," she said. "We were out back, didn't hear the bell."

"It's okay," said Aria, even though Caroline felt woozy.

"Come on in," said Ginny. When Caroline hesitated, she laughed. "We don't bite."

Aria put her hand on Caroline's shoulder and nudged the girl over the threshold.

"Oh hey," Ginny added. "Cool shirt."

chapter 22

ARIA

Aria quickly decided sleepovers were her new favorite thing. Better than cupcakes, or fresh apples, or fall leaves. Sleepovers were made of snacks and laughter, swimming pools and music. And everyone seemed so relaxed.

She was used to being around sad girls, girls twined in smoke and trouble, girls who needed her help. But it was nice, for once, to be surrounded by happy ones. And it helped that those girls seemed to make Caroline happy, too. The more Caroline was around them, the more her smoke seemed to thin.

Aria sat on the lip of the pool, her legs sloshing back and forth in the water. She was wearing a sunshine-yellow bathing suit, and these strange floaties on her arms like little plastic wings (Aria didn't think she needed them, but Ginny's mom had insisted, and they made Caroline smile, so Aria didn't mind, even if she looked a little silly).

Sitting there, Aria felt like a normal girl. Like she belonged. It wasn't something she'd ever wanted before, ever thought of, but she liked it. She made herself stop and remember that it wouldn't last, that she wasn't like the other girls. But that made her sad, and since she didn't want that sadness or worry to rub off on Caroline, she decided to just enjoy the feeling while she could.

Aria stared down at her reflection in the water, squinting at the empty space over the shoulders of her yellow bathing suit. If she made the world blur, she could almost see the start of wings.

And then she heard Caroline laugh — not a tight, nervous sound, but something genuine — and Aria looked up in time to see another tendril of blue smoke disappear.

When they'd first arrived, Caroline wouldn't leave Aria's side. But now she was doing flip turns in the pool with Ginny while Elle, Renée, and Amanda bounced a beach ball between them.

Something tugged in Aria's chest — the feeling that she was in the right and wrong place at the same time — and she knew it was because of Lily. But at least Aria had a plan in motion now. She only hoped it would work.

"Truth or dare!" said Ginny later.

They were all sitting in a pillow fort (Aria and Elle had made it from scratch, not in a magical way, just a "let's use everything we can find around the house" way).

Elle was playing with Aria's hair, and Caroline was sitting cross-legged between Amanda and Renée, and Ginny was perched on a massive cushion.

"Dare," challenged Amanda with a smirk.

"Hmmmm . . ." said Ginny.

"Oh, I know!" said Elle. She whispered in Ginny's ear, and Amanda was instructed to put six marshmallows in her mouth and then call and order a pizza. She couldn't get out the word *cheese*, so she had to hang up, which sent everyone into giggles.

Renée picked truth.

"Do you have a crush on anyone?" asked Elle.

Renée spent the next ten minutes talking about a boy named Jimmy, who was taking her to the dance, and who apparently had the bluest eyes in all of Eastgate. Everyone else seemed to know who he was. Aria simply nodded along.

Ginny boldly chose dare, and had to smear peanut butter on her face and go over to the neighbors' asking for jelly. A boy who couldn't have been more than five or six actually brought her a jar of strawberry jam.

Ginny beamed, victorious, and wiped her face on a towel while the other girls fell over laughing.

Before they were back to Ginny's house, Ginny turned to Aria and said, "Okay, truth or dare?"

Aria came to a stop on the sidewalk and chewed her lip. "Dare."

Ginny flashed a mischievous smile, and pointed to the nearest house.

"Go knock on the door," she said, "and if someone answers, you have to kiss them on the cheek."

The group let out a mixture of gasps and giggles. Aria's eyes widened.

"That's not nice," said Caroline. "You should let her pick again."

"She chose dare!" said Elle.

"Yeah, but —"

"I'll do it," said Aria decidedly.

"Really?" said the girls at once.

"Are you sure?" asked Caroline.

"You don't have to," said Ginny. "I can think up something else."

But Aria shook her head. "No," she said. "It'll be fun." Still, her heart fluttered as she made her way up the front steps. She glanced back and saw the girls looking on with awe. And then Aria turned, and knocked, and waited.

She wondered who would answer (if anyone did), whether it would be an old lady or a little kid or a mom or —

The door swung open. It was a boy. Not just a boy. But a boy with a summer tan and brown hair and green eyes. A boy Aria's age. Aria had met boys her age at Gabby's school, but she hadn't planned on kissing any of them.

"Can I help you?" he said, flashing a smile that made a dimple appear in his cheek. Aria felt her face redden.

"Um," she said.

"You okay?" asked the boy.

"Yeah, I . . ." Aria searched her brain for words. "Can I tell you a secret?" she blurted out.

"Uh, sure?" he said. He leaned in a little, and so did she. And then Aria kissed him on the cheek. The boy pulled back and looked at her with surprise, and Aria felt like her face was on fire. She started to back away. "Sorry," she said. "It was just this silly game and I —"

"Wait," said the boy. Aria stopped. "You forgot something."

"I did?" asked Aria. He motioned her closer, and then he leaned forward and kissed *her* on the cheek. Then he pulled away, smiled, and went back inside.

The door shut, but Aria stood on the front steps, her heart racing, her face hot. For a second, she forgot who she was. What she was. Not in a bad way, or a scary way, but in a strange, wonderful, totally new way. And then she turned back toward the girls, and smiled so wide that the whole evening — street lights and setting sun and all — seemed to glow brighter.

The girls cheered, and Aria gave a sweeping bow.

Several minutes later, when they were all collapsed back in Ginny's bedroom, Aria still hadn't stopped smiling. And then Ginny pulled a pillow into her lap, turned to Caroline, and said, "All right, truth or dare."

Caroline hesitated, smoke curling around her.

And then to Aria's surprise, she took a deep breath and said, "Truth."

Suddenly Ginny got very serious. "Okay," she said. "What happened between you and Lily Pierce?"

chapter 23

CAROLINE

Everyone went quiet.

Caroline felt like she'd been punched in the stomach. The light and happiness began to leak out of the room as Caroline looked from Ginny to Elle, Elle to Renée, Renée to Amanda, and then finally to Aria.

Caroline couldn't read Aria's mind, but her expression seemed to say one thing.

Tell the truth.

All Caroline wanted to do was forget. To put the past behind her and start fresh. But she couldn't. Going forward sometimes meant looking back, and if she really wanted to make new friends, they deserved to know what had happened with her old ones.

So she told them.

About Lily and Erica. About standing up for Whitney, and being kicked out of the group for it.

When she was done, the room stayed quiet. Ginny frowned, and for a second Caroline thought she was mad at her. Then Caroline realized Ginny was mad *for* her. "I can't believe they'd stoop that low," she growled.

"Can't you?" challenged Elle. "They're the meanest girls in school."

"I'm so sorry," said Renée.

"We just figured you two got in a fight," added Amanda.

"We didn't know," said Ginny, squeezing Caroline's shoulder.

"Does *Whitney* know?" asked Elle.

Caroline started to shake her head, when Aria cut in. "Yeah, she knows."

Caroline shot Aria a surprised look.

"And she still hangs out with them?" snapped Ginny. "Why would *anyone* put up with that?"

"Maybe she's scared," Caroline said quietly.

"Maybe she's *crazy*," countered Elle.

"Well," said Ginny decidedly, "if she isn't willing to stand up for herself, that's her problem. Can't help someone who doesn't want to be helped. You did the right thing, Caroline."

"Thanks," said Caroline, hugging a pillow to her chest. She let out a deep breath, and for the first time in weeks, she felt like she could breathe.

Ginny cleared her throat. "Now back to business," she said. "So, Elle, truth or dare?"

That night, when the girls were asleep, a tangle of pajama-ed limbs on the pillow fort floor, Caroline lay there, looking at the ceiling as if it were the night sky. And then, as she gazed up, tiny dots of light — like stars — began to pepper the darkened room.

"Hey, Aria," she whispered in the dark. "Are you doing that?"

"Yeah," Aria whispered back. There was a moment of silence, and then Aria said, "This was really fun." It was strange, the way she said it. Happy and sad at the same time.

"Thank you," said Caroline.

"For what?" asked Aria.

"For everything."

"We're not done yet," said Aria, and Caroline could hear the smile in Aria's voice as the stars began to soften and blink out. "But we're on our way."

Caroline's mom picked them up early the next morning for Saturday school. Caroline was still rubbing sleep from her eyes and pulling her hair back into a messy ponytail as she got in the car, Aria bobbing behind her. Aria didn't look tired at all. If anything, she seemed peppy.

"What's it like?" she asked as they rode to Westgate.

"What's what like?" asked Caroline with a yawn.

"Saturday school," said Aria.

Caroline shrugged. She had never gotten a Saturday school before, so she didn't know what to expect. Would they be sweeping the floors? Picking up trash? Dying of boredom at a desk? The possibilities were endless.

When they got to school, Mr. Cahill was waiting for them in the office. He led them to the gym, where rolls of colored paper and buckets of paint were waiting for them.

Mr. Cahill swept his hand over the crafts and said, "Dance prep."

"We're going to dance?" asked Aria, her face lighting up. "That doesn't seem like much of a punishment."

"No, you're going to *prep* for this week's dance."

Aria considered the gym. "But can we dance while we're prepping?"

160

Mr. Cahill sighed. "Sure," he said. "But don't have too much fun. This is Saturday school after all." He *almost* smiled when he said it. "The theme is 'In the Clouds,' so I need you girls to start painting clouds on the blue paper roll. Think you can handle that?" Aria and Caroline nodded. "Great. I'm going to find coffee."

Mr. Cahill left. Aria started to roll out some of the blue paper. "What a perfect theme," she said. "It was made for you."

"It's weird, isn't it?" said Caroline. The whole school had voted, and she'd been sure they were going to choose something flowery and pink. But Caroline had kept thinking how cool it would be to dance in the sky.

Aria shrugged. "Sometimes things just work out," she said with a mischievous smile.

There was a radio in the corner, and Aria turned it on. Music echoed through the gym while they worked. Soon they were singing along — Aria cheerfully off-key — and laughing, and Caroline was just starting to think Saturday school wasn't so bad at all.

Then the gym doors banged open, and in walked Lily Pierce.

chapter 24

ARIA

Caroline froze. "What is *she* doing here?" she hissed.

Aria shrugged. "Not sure," she said, even though she knew *exactly* what Lily was doing there.

She hadn't turned Lily in for the swimming pool incident (in part because she didn't have proof, and in part because she wasn't sure Ms. Pierce would make Lily come today). But Aria *had* read the entire pamphlet on Westgate's rules. So, all day on Friday, Aria had made sure that Lily broke just enough of the rules to land in Saturday school.

"My phone was turned off!" Lily had told the teacher after history class.

"Then how did it ring during my lecture?" he demanded.

"Mr. Cahill," Lily had said at lunch, aghast, "I swear my shoelaces were black this morning."

"Mhmmm," said Mr. Cahill, "so they just magically turned green."

"I don't know how the popcorn got in my locker," Lily had said later that day, exasperated.

"I could smell it all the way down the hall," said the eighth-grade monitor. "And where did you even find a microwave?"

(That one had kind of been Lily's own fault. She'd brought the bag of popcorn to school herself. Aria had simply made it pop.)

"Three strikes," her mother, the headmistress, had snapped. "What's gotten into you?"

Aria had almost felt guilty for setting Lily up (especially when she saw her face after leaving her mother's office), but Aria had to do *something* to get Caroline and Lily together alone, and in neutral territory.

Now Lily marched over, and, without saying a word or looking at either one of them, she picked up a paintbrush and started making clouds.

"I'm going to go wash my hands," said Aria, holding them up to show they were covered in white paint.

Caroline gave her a look that very clearly said, *Don't leave me here.*

And Aria gave her one back that said *You said this was what you wanted. A chance to talk? So go ahead. Talk.* (Though

Aria wasn't very good at giving people looks, so she wasn't sure that all came across.)

Caroline shook her head. *I changed my mind.*

Aria frowned. *Change it back.*

By this point, Caroline and Aria had been staring at each other for several long moments.

"So go already," said Lily, annoyed.

Aria slipped out into the hall and wiped her hands together, the white paint vanishing. Then she willed herself to disappear. Invisible, she stood on her tiptoes and looked back through the glass insert of the door.

Caroline and Lily were not talking.

They were not talking in that way that said they clearly wanted to — the whole room, not just the smoke, was filled with things they weren't saying. But neither one of them would go first.

A minute later Mr. Cahill came back with a mug of coffee and a newspaper under his arm. When he pushed the gym door open, Invisible Aria followed him inside.

"Miss Pierce," said Mr. Cahill, turning down the music. "I never thought I'd see you here."

"Yeah," grumbled Lily. "Me neither."

Caroline opened her mouth as if to speak, but didn't. She and Lily went back to silently painting puffy white clouds on the blue paper. Aria, still invisible, came up beside Caroline and wrote a word in the wet paint of the nearest cloud.

TALK.

Caroline's eyes widened a little. She glanced over at Lily, but Lily hadn't seen the trick.

"What are you staring at?" asked Lily without looking up.

Caroline blinked. "Can you pass the paint?"

Lily lifted the bucket and dropped it between them. It splashed, dotting both their clothes with white. Lily groaned. Caroline laughed.

"It's not funny," snapped Lily.

Caroline's giggles trailed off. "Do you remember that time," she said, "when your dad was painting the window, and left the bucket on the ladder, and Erica knocked into it?"

Lily rolled her eyes. "Oh god, she was *covered* in red paint."

"She was so worried about her hair. Not her clothes or her shoes or her skin. She was just terrified it would dye her hair."

Lily cracked a smile. "She didn't want to be a redhead."

Caroline started to laugh. This time, Lily did, too. The blue smoke that circled both of them thinned a fraction.

When their laughter trailed away, Lily said, "Hey, do you remember that one time when —"

But she was cut off by the sound of the gym doors banging open, Aria turned to see Erica and Whitney barging inside. Aria groaned inwardly. Caroline grimaced, and to Aria's surprise, *Lily's* smoke began to darken at the sight of the two girls.

"What up, losers?" said Erica loudly, her voice echoing through the gym.

"Language, Miss Kline," warned Mr. Cahill.

"What are you doing here?" asked Lily.

"We came to save you," said Whitney, "from being stuck with trash." The second part she said too low for Mr. Cahill to hear, but Caroline clearly heard.

Aria could see Lily's expression falter. Just for a second. Her mouth opened as if she was going to defend Caroline, but then she put on a stiff smile and said, "Ugh, thanks. Let's get some fresh air." She dropped her paintbrush back in the bucket, splashing flecks of white on Caroline. This time, neither one of them laughed. Anger rolled through Aria, and she had to resist the urge to stick out her foot and trip Lily.

"Can I take a break, Mr. Cahill?" Lily called out. "The smell of paint is making me sick."

Mr. Cahill sighed, and nodded. "Fine," he said. "Ten minutes."

He turned to Caroline. "You can take one, too, if you want."

Caroline's knuckles were white around her paintbrush. "That's okay," she said as Lily and Erica and Whitney vanished through the doors. "I'll stay here."

Mr. Cahill looked around. "Where's Aria?" he asked.

When his back was turned, she flickered into sight.

"I've been here the whole time," she said, cross-legged on the floor.

"Oh," said Mr. Cahill, blinking. "Well, carry on."

Caroline kept painting, even though tears were rolling silently down her cheeks. "I thought . . ." she whispered. "I thought . . . just for a moment . . . we could . . ."

"So did I," said Aria. She really thought, if she could get the two of them alone . . . and for a second, it had worked. Lily's smoke had thinned, and Aria had been able to see a side of Lily she hadn't before. But it wasn't enough.

And when Lily finally came back from her break, she didn't say another word to Caroline.

chapter 25

CAROLINE

All day a cloud hung over Caroline. Somehow getting a flash of old Lily made the new Lily even worse. And the *worst* part was that Caroline could see the old Lily in there somewhere, under all that mean, but she couldn't get her out.

Just when she felt like she'd never shake the dark cloud — did her smoke look the way this felt? — she and Aria got back to her house, paint-streaked and tired, and saw Ginny and Elle waiting for them on the steps.

"There they are, our little rule-breakers," said Ginny.

"Tell us, what's it like to be juvenile delinquents?" teased Elle.

"Messy," said Aria, holding up her paint-covered hands. "We painted clouds for the dance."

"What's the theme again?" asked Ginny.

"The sky," said Aria, and Elle tilted her head to one side.

"Hmm," she said. "That might be tricky to shop for. Ginny and I were going to the mall to look at dresses for the dance. Can you come?"

Standing there with Ginny and Elle, Caroline felt her spirits begin to lift. They didn't care who was most popular. They weren't bullies or nobodies. They were just themselves. Caroline nodded enthusiastically.

"You coming like that?" asked Ginny. "I mean, paint-splattered is a good look."

Caroline laughed. "No," she said. "Let me go inside and change. And actually I need to ask my mom if I can go."

As Caroline suspected, her mom was more than happy to let her go to the mall with new friends. It seemed Saturday school was now forgiven.

Shopping at the mall was a lot of fun, and Ginny and Elle didn't care if the dresses Caroline picked out matched their "color scheme" or not. There were no rules, and for the first time in a long time, Caroline just enjoyed herself without feeling self-conscious. Aria seemed to be enjoying herself, too — she'd never gone shopping before, she explained to Caroline in a whisper. Aria didn't buy a dress for herself — Caroline knew she could summon one up for the dance — but Caroline picked out a shimmery blue one with a poofy knee-length skirt.

By the time Monday rolled around, Caroline wasn't even dreading school.

Lily stayed out of her way, and didn't shoot her dirty glances. In fact, she didn't look at her at all. Erica still glared, of course, and Whitney whispered something harsh under her breath when she and Erica passed Caroline in the hall.

"Ignore them," said Aria, and to Caroline's surprise, she did.

For the first time all year, she had fun in gym. They were playing dodgeball and by some miracle, she got through most of the class without being hit a single time (she suspected she had Aria to thank for that).

"Hey, do you actually go to class when we're not together?" Caroline asked Aria as they walked down the hall together.

"Yeah," said Aria cheerfully. "Well, everything except math." The teacher had claimed that math was a kind of magic, explained Aria, but she remained unconvinced. To her, it just looked like numbers.

"What class do you have now?"

"Math."

"So what are you going to do instead?"

Aria shrugged. "Wander," she said. "Invisible, of course."

"Of course," said Caroline. "Well, have fun. I'll see you at lunch."

She watched Aria go, and then, just as she was rounding a corner, a girl slammed into Caroline *hard*. Hard enough to make her drop the books and papers she was carrying. It was Jessabel.

"You're still nothing," she muttered, then bounced cheerfully off to class. The blow knocked the wind out of Caroline, and the words made it worse, and she crouched in the hall, trying to gather up their things. And then she felt someone kneel down to help.

"Thanks," said Caroline. "You don't have to."

"I know," said the girl. Caroline looked up to see that it was a seventh grader named Jen.

"Hey," said Caroline, straightening. "You're in the science club, right?"

Caroline knew that because in sixth grade Lily had told her to fill Jen's locker with bugs — mostly crickets and a couple of worms, because she liked biology — and Caroline had done it. And she'd laughed along with everyone else when Jen opened the locker. Jen probably hated her. She had every right to.

They hadn't said a word to each other since then. Now Jen gave her a guarded look. "Yeah . . . why?"

Caroline offered a genuine smile. "I was thinking about joining the club."

Jen raised a brow. "*You?*"

"Yeah," said Caroline. "Why not me?"

"It's just, you never struck me as a science nerd."

"I love science," said Caroline. "Astronomy is my favorite, but really, I like all of it. I just never joined before because —"

"Because you were too cool then?" cut in Jen. "And now you're not cool enough for it to matter?"

Caroline cringed. Jen's tone made her want to hide. But she didn't. She had to face the fact that she'd done bad things. "You're right," she said. "I didn't join because I thought it was nerdy and uncool. I didn't know what cool *was*. I always thought being popular was what made you cool. But it's not. Liking something — really liking it — that *is* cool. So I think it's awesome that you like science. I think it's really cool."

Jen considered her a moment, clearly trying to decide if this was some kind of trick. Caroline recognized the distrust. But then Jen pulled a flier out of her bag and handed it over. "We meet after school on Wednesdays," she said.

Caroline brightened. "Do you get to do experiments?" she asked. "Like crystal-growing or how to get the colors in fireworks?"

Jen smiled, this time a real smile. "Yeah," she said. "Last week we got to make our own bouncy balls out of polymer."

"No way," said Caroline. "That's awesome. How did you do it?"

The second bell rang overhead.

"We have English together, right?" asked Jen. Caroline nodded. "Well, walk to class with me; I'll tell you about it. . . ."

chapter 26

ARIA

Instead of going invisible, Aria went looking for Lily.

She'd spent all weekend thinking about what to do, how to get through to her. Now she thought she finally understood what Lily needed to hear.

As Caroline's smoke had thinned, and Lily's hadn't, the pull toward the second girl had gotten stronger. Aria wove through the halls of Westgate to the headmistress's office, and paused outside. The office door was ajar, and she could see Lily standing in front of the headmistress's desk — her mother's desk. Her blue smoke was swirling around her.

"This is unacceptable," Ms. Pierce was saying, waving a test paper. A grade was written on the top in bright red pen: *B.* "I don't know where your head is, but it clearly isn't here. First the infractions —"

"I didn't do any of those —"

"And now this."

"It's just a B, Mom. It's not the end of the world."

"Just a B?" snapped Ms. Pierce. "This isn't *just* a B, because you aren't *just* a student, Lily. You're an example for every girl here at Westgate. I told you when you started here there would be expectations. How do you think it looks when the headmistress's daughter doesn't embody the excellence expected by the school? And for goodness' sake, stand up straight." Ms. Pierce sighed and rubbed her eyes. "Maybe you're spending too much time with your friends, and not enough on your work."

Lily let out an exasperated noise. "It's called a social life! Isn't having one part of being a well-rounded Westgate girl?"

"Don't you take that tone with me."

"What more do you want from me?" snapped Lily. "I run track in the fall. I play tennis in the spring. I'm class president. I'm the most popular girl in this school!"

"Exactly. All eyes are on you. Every girl here should look up to you, should want to *be* you. You owe it to them to be the best example."

"I just —"

"No," Ms. Pierce cut her off. "No excuses."

Lily's shoulders slumped. The bell rang. "Go to class," said her mom. "The last thing you need is an infraction for being late."

Aria felt bad for Lily. No wonder she trying so hard to be in charge. And no wonder she had become a bully. Her mom was one, too. Aria didn't think Lily's mom would change anytime soon. But Lily could. She had to.

Lily pushed the door open, and nearly ran straight into Aria. Her eyes narrowed.

"Why can't you just stay out of my way?" she barked.

"Lily Ann Pierce," warned her mother from the office doorway. "You're going to be late!"

Lily looked back in the office and forced a smile. "I was just talking to Westgate's newest student," she said tightly. "I wanted to make sure she felt welcome."

"I'm sure she does," said Mrs. Pierce. "And I'm sure you two can talk and walk at the same time."

Silently, Lily nodded, and started walking away. Aria followed.

"I'm sorry," Aria said.

"For what?" Lily grunted. "Getting in the way?"

"For your mom," said Aria. The answer seemed to catch Lily off-guard and she glanced at Aria, her face paling. "It's not fair to put that much pressure on you."

"That's not really any of your business," Lily snapped, recovering.

Aria shrugged. She wasn't going to back down. "I couldn't help but overhear, okay? It hurts, doesn't it. Being singled out by somebody. Being picked on." Lily's eyes narrowed as she saw where Aria was going with this. "If you ever want to talk —"

"Why would I ever want to talk to *you*?"

"Because you have to talk to someone," Aria said. Erica and Whitney didn't seem like good listeners. Mimickers, sure, but not listeners. Caroline had been Lily's listener, until Lily had pushed her away. "You can't just bottle everything up and then take it out on others," pressed Aria.

Lily threw her hands up. "I don't get it. What do you *want*?"

"To *help*," said Aria.

"I don't want your help," said Lily. "And I certainly don't need it."

"Do you miss her?" asked Aria.

Lily came to a stop. "Who?"

"Caroline. Do you miss her?"

The blue smoke coiled around Lily's shoulders.

"I know what happened between you two," continued Aria. "I haven't had very many friends, but I don't think friends are supposed to do what you did."

"You don't know anything —"

"I know she stood up to you," said Aria. "And instead of listening, or letting it go, or just saying you were sorry, you decided to ruin her life."

Lily stared at her, wide-eyed.

Guilt. Aria could practically see it woven through the smoke. Guilt, and sadness. But Aria knew now: Lily didn't need a hug. She didn't need support. She needed someone to stand up to her. And maybe that someone needed to be Caroline. But first, Aria could make a few cracks in the armor of *Mean* Lily so that when Caroline *did* stand up to her, the words would get through, and Lily would finally hear, finally listen.

"How dare you talk to me that way?" said Lily. "You are nothing. You are no one."

"The girls at this school aren't nice to you because they like you," said Aria. "They're afraid of you. But I'm not. Nothing you do can hurt me."

Lily clutched her books to her chest. "You think Caroline's your friend," she said, "but she will *always* come running back to me."

"Are you sure about that?" asked Aria. "What happens the day she doesn't? What happens when she realizes she's not afraid of losing you anymore?"

Lily stood there, speechless. Aria thought she might finally have gotten through. Then the bell rang again, and the sound jarred Lily free.

"You are nothing," she said again. "I'll prove it to you."

And with that, she stormed away.

"I think it's time we pick a new target."

Lily and Erica and Whitney were walking to lunch. Lily still walked in front, the other two trailing, but Erica and Whitney's arms were linked, and now and then they passed a secret look between them. A smile. An eye roll.

"Getting soft?" asked Erica.

"No," snapped Lily. "Getting bored. Caroline's no fun anymore. And frankly, this group is lame without her."

"Ouch," said Whitney.

"Harsh," said Erica.

"Honest," said Lily. "But the point is, we need a change."

"Because you're slipping," said Erica. She'd stopped echoing Lily, and started speaking up. She was getting bolder.

"Did you know someone *turned Jessabel in* for being mean?" said Whitney. "It's like they actually care what happens to Caroline."

"It's Aria," snapped Lily. "It's all *her* fault. And that's why we're going to make her the newest target."

"You sure that will work?" challenged Erica. "People seem to like her."

"You think they'll actually freeze her out?" asked Whitney.

"*They're* not going to," said Lily. "*Caroline* is."

Erica raised a brow, and a second later, so did Whitney.

"Ouch," said Whitney.

"Harsh," said Erica.

But they both smiled as they said it. The three girls pushed open the cafeteria doors and vanished within.

For a moment, the hall was empty.

Then the air shimmered and Aria became visible again. She'd heard everything. And she knew what she had to do.

Nothing.

It was up to Caroline now.

Aria took a deep breath, smoothed her skirt, and went to lunch.

chapter 27

CAROLINE

Caroline was halfway through the lunch line when she felt an arm loop through hers, and looked up to see Lily beside her. Caroline tried to pull free, but Lily tightened her grip.

"Hi," said Lily. *Hi*. Like they were still friends.

"What do you want?" asked Caroline.

"Look," said Lily. "We need to talk."

"We were talking, on Saturday. And then you decided to stop."

"I'm sorry."

Two words Lily almost never said, but Caroline didn't buy it.

"I'm sorry about Saturday school," Lily went on, "and I'm sorry about the diving board, and I'm sorry about the pool party last week. That was Erica, not me. She took my phone. I didn't even know about it until I came out and saw them giggling."

"Whatever."

"You don't have to believe me," snapped Lily. "But it's the truth." She waved her free hand. "Anyway, that's not the point."

"What *is* the point?"

"I've been talking to the girls, and we all agree. It's time for you to come back to the group."

Caroline stared at Lily. She didn't know what to say. "Even Erica?" she asked.

"Even Erica," said Lily. Caroline didn't believe her.

"Come on, Car," cooed Lily. "I miss you."

"I miss you, too," said Caroline. The words came out before she even thought of stopping them. And they were true. She did miss Lily. In spite of everything.

"There's just one thing you have to do," said Lily. "To prove you want back in. To show you're one of us."

Caroline's heart sank. "What?"

"If you do it," Lily went on, "then things can go back to the way they were. The way they're supposed to be. Don't you want that?"

Caroline swallowed. Her eyes traveled over the lunchroom. She saw Aria sitting with Ginny and Elle. Aria's back was to her, so she didn't see Caroline standing there with Lily. Caroline remembered how she'd said there were more choices than being a bully or a nobody.

"Well?" pressed Lily.

Caroline frowned. "What do I have to do?"

Lily smiled, and leaned in, and whispered in her ear.

Caroline stood there, clutching her tray.

She could feel Lily and Erica and Whitney watching her, all waiting to see if she would do it. She made her way toward Aria.

The drink on her tray was filled to the brim with an icy red concoction. As she crossed the cafeteria, she had to focus on not spilling it.

Dump it on Aria, Lily had said when she set the drink on her tray. *Dump it on her, and everything will go back to the way it was before.*

When Caroline finally reached the table, she hovered at Aria's shoulder. Aria looked up.

"Hey," said Aria cheerfully. "You going to sit down?"

The other girls at the table looked up, too. Ginny, Elle, Renée, and Amanda. It felt like the whole cafeteria was watching her. Caroline tightened her grip on her lunch tray.

This was it.

The moment of choice.

She took a deep breath.

And then she sat down next to Aria.

As soon as she did, the fear and the stress went out of her. She knew she'd made the right decision. Aria reached over and squeezed her arm, as if she *knew*. Knew what Caroline had thought of doing. Knew what she'd decided *not* to do.

"Hey, Ginny," said Caroline, a little shaky, "can you pass me a —"

A hand came down on her shoulder, hard, and she jumped. When she did, the icy red drink spilled over the table, and the girls all jumped up out of its path. Caroline spun around to find Lily looking furious.

"What do you think you're doing?" she hissed. "This isn't how you get back in the group."

Everyone at the table — everyone in the *cafeteria* — was staring at them. Sixty-two pairs of eyes.

"I don't want to be back in the group," said Caroline. Her voice trembled but she kept going. "I don't want to be your friend anymore, Lily. I don't like the person you've become."

Lily turned red. It started in her cheeks, and spread

across her face and down her neck, and for a moment, Caroline thought she was going to cry.

Erica appeared at Lily's shoulder. "Lily, are you seriously going to let her talk to you like that?" she asked.

"You can't let her do that," Whitney chimed in, appearing on Lily's other side.

"You're supposed to be —"

"Back off," snapped Lily. "Both of you." She turned and stormed out of the cafeteria.

Erica and Whitney stood there, shocked, before slowly retreating back to their own table.

Caroline felt Aria squeeze her arm again. She took a deep breath and turned back to Ginny, and Elle, and the rest of Table 2 watching with a mixture of surprise and approval. She looked down at the icy red slush on everything, and sighed. "We're going to need more napkins."

By the end of the day, everyone in school seemed to know about the lunchroom scene. Caroline hadn't realized how many people *wanted* to stand up to Lily Pierce until girls started coming to thank her. Everyone treated it like a victory . . . so why did Caroline still feel strangely defeated?

"You did the right thing," insisted Aria.

"I know," said Caroline.

"Miss Mason," called Ms. Opeline as they passed her office. "Is everything all right?"

"Yes, ma'am," said Caroline.

"I haven't seen you in a while. No more accidents? No wardrobe malfunctions?"

"No," said Caroline with a smile. She and Aria started to walk away, but Ms. Opeline stepped forward.

"I know it hasn't been an easy year," she said. *You have no idea*, thought Caroline bitterly, before reminding herself that it wasn't Ms. Opeline's fault. Caroline hadn't *told* her. "But I'm glad that things seem to be getting better."

"They are," said Caroline.

"Middle school is . . ." started Ms. Opeline. "Well, actually, the world is full of bullies. But being mean never earns you friends, only enemies. I think that's a hard lesson, don't you?"

Caroline nodded.

"I'm still here," said Ms. Opeline. "If you ever want to talk."

Caroline paused and turned back. "I know," she said. "And thank you."

"Who's that?" asked Aria once they were outside.

"Ms. Opeline, the school counselor."

"Do you ever talk to her?" asked Aria.

"I don't need to talk to her. I have you."

Aria hesitated. "Caroline," she said slowly, "I won't be here forever. You know that, right?" Caroline's gaze dropped to the floor. She hadn't thought about it. Hadn't wanted to. "I told you in the tree house," pressed Aria. "I'll be here until your smoke clears and you don't need me anymore. But then I have to go."

"Why?" asked Caroline. "Why not stay?"

"I don't have a life here," said Aria. "I don't have a family. I have a mission. And once it's over, I have to move on. Just like you do, with your new life. We both have to keep moving forward. But promise me," added Aria, "that if things get hard after I'm gone, you'll talk to Ms. Opeline, or your mom, or your sister, or *someone*. Okay?"

Caroline nodded.

"And hey," said Aria, slinging her arm around Caroline's shoulders. "I'm not gone yet. I have to see what this dance thing is all about."

chapter 28

ARIA

"Keep your eyes closed."

Aria was sitting on Caroline's bed, and Caroline was putting her hair into a French braid for the dance. Aria was excited to see what it would look like.

"There," said Caroline when she was done. "What do you think?"

Aria blinked, looked at herself in the mirror, and beamed.

"It's like I'm someone else," she said.

Caroline smiled. "It's just hair."

"Where did you learn to do that?"

Caroline shrugged. "My sister taught me."

"Oh," said Aria.

"Here," said Caroline. "I'll show you how."

She started to take the braid apart, but Aria stopped her.

"No," she said. "Leave it like this. It's perfect."

Caroline's own hair fell in loose blond waves down her back. Aria thought she looked beautiful in her blue dress.

"What are you going to wear?" Caroline asked.

Aria looked down at her school uniform. She snapped her fingers, and the plaid skirt and polo shimmered and shifted and transformed into a yellow skirt, a red shirt, and a pair of bright blue leggings. Her shoelaces turned violet, and Aria smiled proudly at her handiwork.

Caroline laughed. "You can't wear that."

"Why not?" asked Aria.

"You kind of look like a walking rainbow."

Aria shrugged. "I like rainbows," she said.

Caroline giggled. "Never mind," she said. "You look like you."

"Caroline," her mom called up, sounding happy. "Your friends are here."

Ginny and Elle were waiting on the porch. They met up with Renée and Amanda, and then they all went out for pizza, which Aria quickly decided was her new favorite food.

When they got to the gym, Aria was amazed by how the massive room had changed, transformed from wood and bleachers into a giant stretch of sky. Bundles of white balloons were everywhere, and painted clouds hung from every

rafter. Streamers in sunset colors ran back and forth overhead. Aria loved it.

The gym was full of Westgate girls and Eastgate boys.
Elle, Ginny, Renée, and Amanda immediately started dancing. Aria wanted to join in but she noticed Caroline looking
around, her expression a little tense, her thin blue smoke
swirling. Aria knew she was looking for Lily.

Then Erica and Whitney strolled in, arm in arm, followed by Jessabel. The three of them were wearing matching
pink dresses.

And Lily wasn't with them.

"Where's Lily?" asked a girl with shiny black hair as the
trio passed her by.

Whitney giggled. "Probably still waiting for us."

Erica shrugged and said, "She couldn't keep up, so she
got left behind."

"About time," said Jessabel. Together, the three girls
strode onto the dance floor.

Aria sighed. She needed to leave, and she was about to
make an excuse, when Caroline beat her to it.

"Come on," she said. "Let's go find Lily."

Aria's shadow put them out across the street from Lily's house, under the branches of the tree house tree. Lily was sitting on the front porch, her knees pulled up to her chest. She was wearing a purple dress, and picking at the hem while tears streamed down her face.

Aria stayed behind — far enough to give them space, close enough to hear — as Caroline crossed the yard, made her way up the front steps, and sat down beside her ex-best friend.

When Lily saw Caroline, her thick smoke began to ripple.

"Are you happy now?" muttered Lily.

"No," said Caroline.

"Did you come here to gloat? To rub it in my face? Congratulations, Caroline Mason, you're popular and I'm not."

"That's not why I came. I wanted to see if you were okay."

"Why do you still care?"

Caroline sighed and pulled her knees up. "I never stopped caring, Lily. Even when you were horrible."

Lily wiped her face with the back of her hand. "You said you didn't want to be friends with me."

"I don't," said Caroline. "I don't know if we *can* be friends again. But you still matter to me. You always will."

Caroline dug her hand into her skirt and pulled out the silver half circle necklace. Lily's eyes widened, and then she pulled her own pendant from beneath the collar of her dress.

"I'm sorry, Car," Lily whispered. "It wasn't supposed to be this way. None of it was."

"But it is," said Caroline. "So what are you going to do now?"

Lily shook her head. "I don't know."

Caroline stood up, and put the necklace back in her pocket. "Come to the dance," she said.

"I can't," said Lily.

Caroline crouched down to look Lily in the eyes. "Why not? Because they hurt your feelings?" She shook her head. "If you don't go, you're letting them win," she said. "Besides, we spent all that time painting clouds. Don't you want to see them? They look amazing."

Caroline straightened and held out her hand. "Come on, Lily."

Lily looked up. Then she reached out, and took Caroline's hand.

As she did, her smoke *finally* began to thin.

Aria smiled. She knew it. Lily didn't need her help. She needed Caroline's.

"But how are we going to get to the dance?" asked Lily, looking around. Her parents didn't seem to be home, and Caroline's already thought she was at the dance.

Aria stepped forward. "I have a way," she said. "But there's something I should probably tell you first."

Aria wasn't sure Lily believed her, even after the trip through her shadow door to the school.

"*How* — how — how did you do that?" stammered Lily, as the three girls stepped out of the light-filled shape and onto the path in front of the gym.

"I told you," said Aria for the fifteenth time. "Guardian angel."

"No way," said Lily for the fifteenth time.

"Way," said Aria.

"Way," said Caroline.

Lily looked up at the gym. Fear flickered across her face, and what was left of her smoke coiled nervously around her shoulders. But Caroline took her hand and gave it a small squeeze.

"Come on," she said. "There are some pretty cool girls at this school. I'll help you meet a few."

Aria followed Caroline and Lily up the stairs, watching as the blue smoke around them got thinner, and thinner, and thinner. By the time the two girls stepped into the gym, it was totally gone.

Aria felt something cool on her wrist, and looked down to see a new feather charm twinkling on her bracelet. It was actually two feathers, linked together on the interlocking rings. When Aria shook her wrist, the charms jingled faintly, like far-off bells.

There was only one ring left to fill, and she could feel it tugging at her. This was her least favorite part. Even though she knew she'd done her job and made Caroline and Lily better, and all of that made her happy, that also meant it was over.

It was an ending, and endings were always sad.

But they were just as important as beginnings. And somewhere else, another girl was waiting for Aria's help.

So Aria watched Caroline and Lily slip into the crowd of the dance.

And then her shadow flared, and she stepped backward, into the light.

chapter 29

CAROLINE

Although Caroline had a nice time at the dance, she kept looking for Aria, afraid that she had left without saying good-bye. As soon as the dance was over, Caroline hurried home, and sighed with relief when she found Aria sitting in the tree house, legs dangling over the open window edge.

"There you are," said Caroline, breathless from climbing up the ladder. "Why did you leave the dance?"

Aria swung her legs back inside. "Because it was time," she said.

"It wasn't even eight. There was still an hour left."

Aria shook her head. "That's not what I meant," she said. "How was the dance?"

Caroline smiled. "It was good. Ginny and Elle weren't too thrilled to see Lily, but they were polite to her. And I wish you'd stayed to see Erica's face . . ."

She trailed off, and a silence fell between them.

"Caroline," said Aria, "it's time for me to go."

"Go where?"

Aria held up the bracelet so she could see the newest feather charm. Caroline paled. "Stay," she pleaded. "Everything is so much better with you here."

"You don't need me anymore," said Aria. "And we all have to move forward."

Caroline felt her chest tighten. "Promise me you'll come back."

Aria smiled. "I promise I'll try. But only if you promise me something."

"What's that?"

"That you'll never go back. Not to the way things were. Mean is easier than nice, and I know it's hard, and it'll only get harder, but promise me if you're ever faced with being a bully or a nobody again, you won't choose bully."

Caroline smiled. "You act like those are the only two options," she said, echoing Aria's own words.

Aria beamed, and threw her arms around Caroline.

"So, where are you going?" asked Caroline when she pulled away.

Aria shook her head. "I won't know until I get there."

"Caroline?" called a voice from the street. It was Lily.

"You'd better go," said Aria. "So should I."

Aria smiled and snapped her fingers, and the cushions, the star lights, and all the little decorations she'd summoned to make the small space cozy disappeared. She and Caroline stood there a moment, two girls in an empty wooden box up in the branches of an old oak tree.

Caroline saw Aria's shadow fidget beneath her feet.

"All right," said Aria. "All right."

She tapped her shoe, and the shadow turned on like a light.

"Good-bye, Caroline," she said.

"Good-bye-for-now," corrected Caroline.

Aria smiled, and nodded, and disappeared.

Caroline snuck back to the tree house later that night, after everyone was in bed.

She climbed the ladder, half expecting, fully hoping to find Aria there again, sitting in a sea of pillows.

But Aria was gone. She'd watched her go.

Caroline sat cross-legged on the floor. Even though Aria and her decorations were gone, Caroline still felt as if she was there, somehow. She couldn't explain it. She looked up through the branches at the twinkling stars.

"Things are going to get better," she said aloud, as if Aria could hear her. Maybe she could. Caroline still didn't know exactly how guardian angels worked.

"After you left," she went on, "Lily and I went out to the trampoline, and we just talked. Finally. About everything. About the last month and the last year and how it all got out of hand. And she said she was going to talk to her mom, about all the pressure she was putting on her. I hope Mrs. Pierce listens. I told Lily she could always talk to Ms. Opeline, too." Caroline sighed. "I don't think she and I can ever be best friends again, not the way we were before. I know we can't go back. But I hope we can go forward. All things go forward, right?" she said, remembering Aria's words. "It's science."

Caroline got to her feet and was about to go, when she noticed the photo of her and Lily. It had slipped to the floor, but when she picked it up, she saw that the blue lines Aria had drawn around them were gone. Instead, a small blue stick figure of a curly-haired girl was drawn between them, with her arms wrapped around both.

Caroline broke into a smile, pocketed the picture, and went home.

chapter 30

ARIA

Aria came back one day at lunch.

Caroline didn't know it. She was sitting at Table 2, with Elle on one side and Ginny on the other. Jen, who was in the science club with Caroline, was sitting across from them, and they were all talking about a movie they had seen.

Caroline wasn't at the center of the universe, but she had an orbit. And she seemed genuinely happy.

Aria watched as she twisted in her seat and started talking to a girl at the table behind her. A girl with black curls and pale skin and a pretty smile. Aria noticed that for once, Lily's smile wasn't fake or forced. She and Caroline leaned their heads together and shared a secret, a comment, a joke, and then they turned back to their separate tables, separate lives.

Over at Table 7, Erica threw her head back and gave a

sharp laugh, and shot a dirty look at another girl across the room. Whitney and Jessabel mimicked her.

Some things didn't change.

There would always be an Erica or a Jessabel or a Whitney, girls who wanted to be on top, and would do anything to get there. But for every one of them there was a Ginny, or an Elle, or a Caroline.

Girls who found a way to be themselves.

Aria stood there watching until the bell rang and the girls put away their trays and filed off to class. She followed behind Caroline, a small pang of sadness in her chest. If she were still here, they'd be going to science class together. Instead, Caroline had her arm looped through Jen's. But once, Caroline glanced back, and Aria wondered if she could feel her there, trailing like a shadow, or if she was just remembering.

Caroline disappeared into the classroom. As the door swung shut, Aria reached out and brought her fingers thoughtfully to the wood. Her hand fell away, and she smiled at her handiwork.

The classroom door was now *covered* in stars. Just a little something for Caroline to see when class was over.

Aria's shadow fidgeted at her feet. *All right*, Aria thought. She didn't belong here anymore.

She still had work to do.

Turn the page for a sneak peek at Aria's next adventure:

everyday angel #3:

Last Wishes

The shadow took shape on the curb outside.

It grew out of nothing, tucked in the dark between two streetlights, so no one saw it happen. No one saw the trace of wings above the shadow's shoulders, and no one saw a twelve-year-old girl with red hair and a blue charm bracelet rise out of the pool of light.

No one *saw* Aria step out of nothing and into the world, but there she was. In a new place for the third time.

The last time.

Aria felt a flurry of excitement. One more girl, one more mission, and she would have her wings.

She exhaled, her breath making a cloud in front of her. How strange. It was much colder here than the last place she'd been, and she shivered and pulled her coat close around her before she even realized she was *wearing* a coat.

Once again, Aria had no idea where she was.

In the distance there was a cluster of tall buildings. From here, they looked small enough to fit in the palm of her hand, but she could tell they must be very, very large. A *city*.

And then she heard music. It was coming from the building to Aria's right. Its marquee announced that the Northeast Division Regional Championship — whatever that was — was going on inside. Aria smiled; she could tell that this was where she was supposed to be.

The lobby was crowded, boys and girls hurrying around in strange and wonderful costumes. They wore glitter and make-up and gossamer, but no one was marked by blue smoke.

The music was coming from an auditorium, and Aria nudged the door open and slid inside.

Onstage, a blonde girl in a green dress was dancing. She was tall and pretty, and her motions were elegant in a practiced way. Aria watched her leap and turn across the stage, landing in a pose just as the music ended. A panel of judges at a table in the front row scribbled on their papers.

And then the crowd grew quiet, and Aria's gaze drifted back to the stage, and she saw her.

The girl padded to the center of the stage in silence. She was pretty, her dark skin dusted with gold and her black hair pulled back into a bun. She was dressed in a shimmering gold leotard with a simple gold frill of skirt, and she glittered from head to toe beneath the bright light.

The only thing that didn't match her outfit was the ribbon of blue smoke coiling around her shoulders.

Caitlin, Mia, Libby, and Hannah became best friends forever at camp, but now they have to go their separate ways. Luckily, they have a very special charm bracelet to share. As they mail it back and forth, each girl will receive it just when she needs it the most!

SCHOLASTIC
scholastic.com

Available in print and eBook editions.

CHARMED1